UNVEILING

Also written by Willard N. Carpenter

Secrets of the Son series

Prodigal

UNVEILING
Secrets of the Son Book II

Willard N. Carpenter

This book is a work of fiction and any resemblance to persons, living or dead, or places, events or locales is purely coincidental. The characters are productions of the author's imagination and used fictitiously.

Mary in the darkness of her illness sees light in the unveiling of Samuel's past.

1 Samuel 17: 45-47 KJV

45   Then said David to the Philistine, Thou comest to me with a sword, and with a spear, and with a shield: but I come to thee in the name of the LORD of hosts, the God of the armies of Israel, whom thou hast defied.

46   This day will the LORD deliver thee into mine hand; and I will smite thee, and take thine head from thee; and I will give the carcases of the host of the Philistines this day unto the fowls of the air, and to the wild beasts of the earth; that all the earth may know that there is a God in Israel.

47   And all this assembly shall know that the LORD saveth not with sword and spear: for the battle is the LORD's, and he will give you into our hands.

To those who made the ultimate sacrifice.

Acknowledgements

- My brother Dom and his friend Harry, who inspired the telling of this story.
- Sherry Gore for visiting us at Zerns farmer's market in Gilbertsville and allowing us to collaborate and have a little fun with my 'family' visiting you and yours in Florida.
- The Citadel, the Military College of South Carolina / Charleston, S.C.
- Fort Bragg, North Carolina. For what the men of SOC and 1st SFG op det Delta do quietly on a daily basis for freedom.
- To my Son Mark, 2nd lieutenant, U.S. Army and the many men and woman who have preceded him in what he will one day do. Fly UH 60 Blackhawk Medevac. And to those crews who risk all as I write.
- To my Son Matt, (Pastor Matt) for your continued help in biblical texts, and your inspiration of my writing in faith.
- To my Daughter Lindsay, my sun shine in life. For sharing and continuing to teach me about children.

- To the quiet community of God's traditional people of the New Testament, whom I love and respect, the Amish.
- My wife Michele, this has brought me to many a place of shared tears and smiles with you. I shall never forget!
- My new team, consisting of:

Michele R. Carpenter, Nurse Educator:
Editorial

Eric Eidle, EIT, President and Editor, The Boyertown Company, Inc.
The Boyertown Bulletin:
Technical Support

Ovi Dogar, Absolute Covers:
Cover design.

Forward

I am sitting here in Fort Lee Lodging writing chapter 17, 18, and 19 when I decided I would like to add to this forward.

I had spent the day at a round table, sitting on a wooden dining room chair at my daughter's and son-in-law's temporary military home, a military hotel of sorts.

The 5th floor where I sit overlooks a barracks area. In the distance can be seen the United States Army museum of 'Woman in the Army'. Michele and I had visited this museum today. It was both interesting and at times emotionally moving as we looked at those women who had given their lives for their country.

Ironically I had written these three Fort Bragg chapters while here visiting our daughter. Though I know what life is like on a post, this did certainly help with writing about the army, while here.

You may wonder what our life on a United States Army Post is like. First thing in the morning, we started with bugle calls 1st was first call, then reveille. We usually slept through these.

What woke us up would be formations of men and women running to cadence. We would get up in time to see the stragglers falling behind on the closed off road below us.

Afterward, as in any city, the post would come alive with cars trucks bicycles and walkers. The only difference is that the majority of folks wear uniforms. As I'm writing this two soldiers in uniform are walking by below on the sidewalk.

We sadly leave here for the last time within the hour. Our daughter will come home for a weekend, and then she with her husband 2nd lieutenant Eli A. will move to Fort Lewis, Washington.

Well Lindsay just walked out the door to work and with some welling of my own eyes it is time to end this at an appropriate place where I pick up with my meeting with Samuel.

After our initial meeting Samuel and I would meet many more times. Some of those times we, our wives and ourselves would sit down over dinner or supper. Other times we would go riding, then other times Sam and I would go over to French Creek State Park to shoot, something we both enjoy doing.

It came time to sit down and write this book. I invited Sam to a working breakfast, where we got a private room at the Shady

Maple Smorgasbord. This is a favorite place for both of us.

We would start out by eating with me going to get my favorite, a western omelet with white American cheese on the inside. Sam always gets his favorite creamed chipped beef on toast.

If anyone of you spent time in the military, it is S.O.S. That would be for any military. I'm using the initials sos because this is a Christian read.

I love sos for breakfast but never had it at Shady Maple Smorgasbord simply because I like omelet's better. We both like bacon and would find ourselves meeting there and laughing about who got more bacon. Trust me it was a lot.

Samuel liked potatoes; I would get fruit, usually melons. He would get water and I would have OJ. We both had coffee. This is where we would start to work, usually on the second cup of coffee.

I carry this lap top that I'm working on now, worthless as far as the frills, but great for word processing on the move. I just have to plug it in where I sit. We got a big table near a wall and went at it.

Samuel loved to talk and would go into great detail. I found myself writing highlights and outlining as we went.

When we started we didn't know how Prodigal was going to go. We both agreed that the story being told was more important than how anyone person wanted it told.

As a rule, I wanted to start this book with a forward. I wanted to speak about Samuel and his family in the present, updating the reader about his life only because I know that the reader would want to know.

The Prologue is where I start the book in the first person from Samuel's perspective. We had a good time regarding this.

When I got word from an agent that she would not accept a book where the protagonist spoke in the first person, he scoffed.

"Protagonist huh, never heard this. I have been an antagonist," said Samuel, while laughing with a cup of coffee in his hand.

"What do you think, what do you believe, what do you want to do," he questioned seriously. He cared about what I was doing.

"I want to do things my way, I want to do things out of the box and unexpected. I want to give the reader something different to read if only I reach one reader and have a positive effect on their life," I told him.

He simply said, "Jah, then that is the mission, Sergeant Carpenter, though I feel very strongly that more than one person is going to read your book," he smiled.

Samuel Hersberger is a cut to the chase type of personality. He believes what he believes.

No one intimidates him in thinking otherwise or makes him feel guilty. He is friendly and approachable until someone is insulting then he keeps that English far from him. He is a humble man, he doesn't like arrogance. He is not what you would have expected when meeting him. He is quiet yet he is commanding not only of physical stature but also in the way he is in charge of his way of life. I have never seen him yell except to get above the din of life on a ranch.

Regardless of what anyone thinks of Samuel Hersberger, he is who he is without apology. No one owes him a thing. He owes no one. He has paid for his beliefs with his blood.

In this book, we bring the relationship between my wife, Michele and Mary into perspective. They share a very special bond.

They have spoken to each other a lot regarding what the two of them have in common and what they have experienced, each individually.

Michele shares this with you in 'A Special word from Michele Carpenter, RN MSN Education'. She shares with you from her own perspective about her stroke and with understanding of what Mary had gone through during the same time period.

Though this book is a Novel, what she writes about is real; we want to bring to light what so many in the world do not understand of what they went through. As a nurse I believe she has done this.

Mary is a very happy woman, who today lives 90% of the time new order Amish the other 10% English.

The English part is broken up between cooking, I taught her how to make hoagies. She wears jeans for horseback riding.

The important part for her is that she is her husband's friend and partner. She is not afraid to give her opinion, and Samuel welcomes it.

They love each other very much and it is evident in the way they look at each other and hold hands after these many years. They are for all intents and purposes still on their honeymoon.

The children will never go thru any form of rumspringa as Samuel or Mary had known it. The children are much more open regarding their lives and dreams while speaking to their parents.

When speaking of their future, they are encouraged to seek out Gods calling in their lives, to find themselves where God wants them to be.

"God is where you will find true happiness, jah," Samuel would say constantly, to all five children. Samuel is more concerned that they find themselves with God whether that be amongst the English or Amish. Five, yes they have five children now. Sarah was added to the fold three years after Christopher. The boys all work the ranch, the girls help their mother. They are respectful, kind, and most importantly loving. They are all strong in character as their parents are.

A Special Word From: Michele Carpenter RN, MSN, Education

My name is Michele Carpenter. As mentioned earlier, I have had an experience similar to Mary that I would like to share.

As a nurse and educator, I am keenly aware that one's health status can change in a moment with no warning signs. When this occurred to me, despite my education and 30 years of nursing experience, I did not immediately seek the medical attention I needed.

I waited, and the results could have potentially been irreversible and devastating. Mary was fortunate that she had Samuel present to advocate for her. Please take a moment to read my story.

As a young child, I was happy, healthy and active. When not in school, I played on the community softball team and enjoyed gymnastics and skating.

My favorite day of the school year was "Olympic Day" when, after singing "Let There Be Peace on Earth" with the rest of the school body, I was able to participate in the same events that I watched the Olympic athletes participate in on television.

I excelled in the high jump, despite my very small stature. I delighted hearing the spectators gasp, as I would dive head first over the bar.

Gym was also a class that I looked forward to, despite the suits we had to wear and the required shower at the end. I held the school record for the highest amount of chin-ups performed by both genders.

However, the one activity I dreaded during gym class was the long distance run. I always found myself needing to walk the last half of the course, due to being short of breath. In fact, any aerobic activity that required any type of endurance was difficult for me.

I began to develop headaches, as an early adolescent. During a routine physical exam, I described my headaches to the physician. I also explained that I was always cold, which seemed totally unrelated at the time, but it was severe enough to necessitate me sitting in front of the heat vent at my home each night to complete my homework assignments.

While auscultating my heart, the physician heard an atypical heart sound called a systolic click.

He sent me for an ultrasound of the heart and I was diagnosed with a prolapsed mitral valve. I asked him later if that was the reason I had problems with my endurance as a child or why I was always cold. He described that the prolapsed heart valve would not have anything to do with my endurance or feeling cold.

He also told me it would be important for me to take antibiotics prior to any invasive medical or dental procedures for the rest of my life, to prevent a cardiac infection.

I also consulted a neurologist with regard to the headaches. Several tests were performed to rule out serious neurological pathology, but nothing was found.

Based on the description of the headaches, I was diagnosed with migraines and prescribed analgesics to help relieve the pain and accompanying nausea and vomiting.

In an effort to determine the etiology for my complaints of feeling cold, I underwent several blood tests to determine if my thyroid and pituitary gland were functioning properly.

They affect metabolism and help regulate body temperature. All was well, so I went on with my life, just thinking I was one of those individuals who were always cold. Needless to say, I owned many socks and sweaters.

As a young adult, my migraines became more severe and frequent. A few more visits to neurologists and additional tests resulted in nothing.

I was prescribed several different medications to try to help manage the pain. At one point, I was prescribed a medication to help prevent them, but to no avail.

As the years went by, the frequency and severity of my headaches became worse. I was now on migraine medication that needed to be administered by injection.

I felt like there was no hope in sight and I believe that the chronic pain actually changed my outlook on life. Rather than enjoy each day, I would feel pressure on a day I was migraine free to accomplish everything I could, because the next day I might be incapacitated.

The headaches caused me to miss days from work and put a strain on my family. It was a difficulty working full time and raising a family with three young children.

Feeling cold all the time, particularly my feet, was now part of my life. At night my feet would be so cold, they would hurt. Taking a hot bath was part of my nightly routine, followed by squeezing them between my husband's legs while sleeping.

Despite my challenge I was thankful that the migraines were my only health problem and for my supportive husband.

On my 43rd birthday, a Friday morning in early September, I was racing around the house, as usual and decided to slip out to a couple of stores before my children awoke.

It was Labor Day weekend and I was excited. Upon my husband's return from work we had planned to go out to dinner to celebrate my birthday and then Hershey Park first thing Saturday morning with the children.

As I exited the house, I noticed that my car was blocked in by another vehicle, which had a manual transmission, one that I was not able to drive.

Since there was plenty of room, I decided to back around it as I had done many times in the past. Upon turning the ignition, I began to feel dizzy.

I contributed it to running around and not eating breakfast. In the back of my mind, I thought that it could be the beginning of an aura that I would get prior to developing a migraine.

I pulled around the car that was blocking mine, but rather than it being instinctive, as it was in the past, I had to think about every turn of the wheel.

By the time I was in the street, my dizziness was severe and I was fearful that I was having a cerebral vascular accident (CVA) also known as a stroke or brain attack.

I remember looking into my rearview mirror, to see if I had a facial droop, a sign of a CVA, which I did not. I was too dizzy to drive, so I decided to pull back up into the driveway.

As I approached the top of the drive way, I had to concentrate to lift my right foot to apply the brake. I came very close to driving through the garage door.

I do not remember putting the car in park, but I do remember struggling to turn off the ignition with my right hand.

Once it was off, I did not have function in my right arm or hand so I rotated my shoulder inward to toss the keys into my left hand.

I contemplated beeping my car horn in an effort to awaken my sleeping children, but the fear of them finding me lifeless in the car motivated me to move forward.

I opened my car door in an effort to make it inside the house. My dizziness had somewhat subsided, but as I attempted to walk toward the front door of my home, my right leg felt as if it weighed 1000 pounds.

I tried to manually lift it with my right hand, but found that it was limp and not able to move. I struggled my way to the door, dragging my right leg.

I remember worrying about how bad I must have looked and embarrassed that one of my neighbors may be seeing me in this state. Now that I'm looking back, it really seems silly.

I opened the front door with my left hand and once inside, considered calling my children. Instead, concerned that seeing me in this condition would alarm them, I saw the couch in the living room and decided if I could just make my way over to it I could lie down and rest.

After doing so for approximately 15 minutes, I tested the limbs on my right side to see if there was any improvement. My grasp was returning and I could independently move my right foot. About 10 minutes later, I felt better and in fact, seemed to be moving normally

At that time, I am not sure if my judgment was impaired or I was simply in denial, but I arose and went about my day running errands as if nothing had happened.

Looking back now, I still do not know why I did not seek immediate medical attention as I advise my patients and students.

I was concerned, but considering my age and the fact that I had no significant medical history, convinced myself that it could not be serious.

My thoughts were that the worst it could be was a transient ischemic attack (TIA). It presents as symptoms of a CVA but without permanent brain damage.

I considered telling my husband, when he returned from work, but chose not to, because a trip to the hospital would alter our weekend plans.

That evening, we went to dinner to celebrate my birthday and then to Hershey Park with the children, the next morning, as planned.

We had a lot of fun at the amusement park and rode many of the rides, including the wild mouse.

On Monday, Labor Day, we enjoyed a picnic and swimming at my parents' home.

That evening, I told my husband, also a nurse, what had happened. He encouraged me to see a physician.

The next day from work, I called for an appointment. I was seen that evening in the office. After being scolded by the physician for not calling 911, I was ordered a series of testing including a CAT Scan and MRI.

On Wednesday evening, after work, I went for the CAT scan. The MRI was not scheduled until Friday. Thursday evening I received a call from the physician.

She started off saying, "I don't know how to tell you this. Oh my God and you are so young." Then she continued, "You have had a stroke."

I was shocked. I responded, "It must have been a very small stroke, because I am fine now."

She replied, "No it was quite large. It was in your cerebellum, the part of the brain that affects balance and coordination. Be sure to have the MRI done and follow-up with a neurologist."

That was the day that my life changed forever!

My visit to the neurologist caused me a great deal of anxiety. I remember staying up the entire night before, anticipating the questions he would ask me.

Those same questions I had heard neurologists ask countless patients with neurological deficits under my care. Those same questions I would teach my students to ask their patients during their assessments.

During the visit, he showed me the CAT scan and MRI films. It was clear, even to the untrained eye that there was a part of my brain that was damaged and would be forever.

Following the visit, where he was unable to find any deficits, he ordered a series of tests, additional consultations and a handful of medications that I was required to take on a daily basis.

The visit triggered a whirlwind of tests and appointments with specialists all over the area, including hematologists, cardiologists and other neurologists.

I was prescribed both oral and injectable medication and it seemed as though each visit to a new specialist added another. I was on a considerable amount of anticoagulant medications, to prevent blood clot formation to help prevent another stroke, so I had to have blood drawn every day or two to monitor its levels.

Sleep was also very difficult. I found that the night prior to the neurologists visit would not be my only sleepless night.

The CVA happened so quickly, without warning and no knew why. I was afraid to go to sleep. I would think What if I was to have another while I was sleeping and the outcome was not as good?

Despite everything that was happening I maintained my full time job and worked hard to be a good wife and mother. It was taking a toll on my entire family. It was reflected in my children's grades in school and my husband's work attendance.

As it turns out, cardiology found the answer to the now long unanswered question as to why the CVA occurred. One of the tests that I underwent was an ultrasound of the heart.

The results were normal; in fact, they did not see the prolapsed mitral valve that I was told I had so many years before.

Following that test, they decided to perform another test called a trans esophageal echocardiogram (TEE) so they can visualize the back of the heart.

The physician indicated to me prior to the test that he anticipated that the results would be normal. It required me to have conscious sedation, so I would be able to follow directions during the test, but not remember it when I awoke.

I remember gagging on the spray they used for the back of my throat to numb it, then nothing. When I opened my eyes, the cardiologist was looking down at me.

The first thing he said to me was, "You have a hole in your heart." I thought I was dreaming. I asked him to tell my father who was in the waiting room, so I could do a reality check later. My husband could not be there since he had already missed time from work taking me to the multitude of other appointments.

Once aroused, the cardiologist informed that he believed this to be the cause of my CVA. He told me that not only did I have a patent foramen ovale, a hole in my heart between the two upper chambers; I also had a atrial septal aneurysm, which is characterized by excessive mobility of the atrial septum, the dividing wall between the two upper chambers.

He suspected that a blood clot formed in this area and traveled to my brain.

I was told that I would be required to take medications to help prevent my blood from clotting for the rest of my life.

When I asked about closing the hole, he expressed that it would be open heart surgery and did not see it as an option.

After hearing the news, I did some independent research and found that there were clinical trials being done, where some people were having their PFO's closed by using a cardiac catheter.

I visited another cardiologist for a second opinion regarding the closure. He told me that he would close it if I had another CVA and the percentage of my chances of that was 20%. I could not believe what I was hearing. Wait until I had another CVA? What was he thinking?

A few weeks later I learned of a conference in center city Philadelphia on the latest interventions in the care of stroke patients.

I registered and attended.

At the conference, neurologists and cardiologists presented the results of the various clinical trials they were performing. One of the clinical trials, which intrigued me, was headed up by the Department of Neurology.

Three groups of patients were randomly assigned. One group was placed on aspirin therapy, one was on Coumadin, an anticoagulant to help prevent clot formation and the other group was having their PFO's closed by the utilization of a cardiac catheter.

Following the neurologists presentation, a cardiologist presented graphic illustrations of the reduction in recurrent strokes after PFO closure.

He also pointed out that there was a higher incidence of PFO's among migraine suffers. I felt like he was talking about me!

I scheduled an appointment with the chief of neurology and visited him the next week. He encouraged me to consider joining the clinical trial and sent me home with a packet of papers.

I considered it, but did not want to be randomly placed in a group. I wanted the hole in my heart closed.

My next visit was to the cardiologist who was participating in the clinical trial by performing the closures on the group of patients that had been randomly selected for that intervention

He encouraged me to join the trial but could not guarantee that I would be in the group that would undergo the closure procedure. I told him that I did not want to join the trial because I wanted the hole closed.

When he asked why, I told him that I had attended the conference and saw the evidence that stroke risk declines with closure. He agreed to close the hole.

Three days before Christmas, that same year. I was admitted to a University Hospital in Philadelphia to have the procedure.

After my overnight admission, I was home with my family. Amazingly, now eight years later, I have had no further neurological incidences and my migraines are virtually nonexistent.

I have found through researching the evidence from current clinical trials that there is a significant correlation between PFO's and migraines and that many migraine sufferers who have PFO's closed, experience fewer migraines.

My feet are also warm as toast and I am now warming my husband's, between my legs, as his feet are getting cool with age.

I thank God every day for giving me a second chance at life and for turning a potentially tragic event into a healing experience and a blessing.

Prologue

It has been 10 years since Mary's illness. Since that time I have retired from my other 'business'.

Those years leading up to my daed's death were, when looking back, good years. I now have no regrets. I have put my relationship with my father into perspective, and to rest in my mind, heart and soul. I am certain he would agree.

I have settled into a routine on the ranch. Looking back during Mary, our kinner and my 'exciting year', we like to call it; we have found that God was with us during the entire time.

Without Mary's stroke we would not have discovered the hole in her heart. Now with that hole repaired Mary's quality of life has improved 100 fold. This is what we consider a quiet gift from God.

She no longer suffers from migraines as she had before. Her feet are now warmer than mine. I'm certain that has something to do with all that bacon I eat, even though my age has a large part to do with it also.

Mary and I have come to know that life amongst the English is not where we want our kinner and ourselves to be. At the same time, it is not in any sense evil as some would lead us to believe.

We choose to live as we do. It is what we know. It is a peaceful existence. It is an existence that does not depend on the outside world in any way. Though I collect a comfortable retirement, we do not depend upon it.

Our Lord and Savior is our constant companion. We do not visit him during times of crises only. We do not visit him for our wants.

We keep our heavenly father with us as a constant. We chat with him at any time as we would if our earthly father may be with us physically.

There are times when we may want quiet and have just some quiet time with each other. This is when we would go to our quiet place and know his peace.

Our strength is our God and our faith. Our strength is staying within our community with steadfastness, caring and most importantly, love.

This life we live is not to be confused with ignorance for we know from generations before us those lessons they learned. Yes we know.

It is not to be confused with cowardess for we face all those things that the English face on a daily basis. We face pain. We face death. We face need. We face uncertainty. The difference is, we face these things with God.

We are not afraid of war; we choose to fight a greater enemy. Where our English brothers and sisters fight a physical war against a seen enemy, we fight an invisible war against an unseen enemy. An enemy much more pervasive than any terrorist this land could ever see.

The enemy we fight, the evilness of Satan, is the champion of those who would do intentional harm to innocence. He is the champion of those you call our enemy and war against. We fight the same wars, only in a different way.

We fight in a quiet way. We fight daily and nightly. We fight outside the vision of those who would look on in wonderment.

We resist, we resist temptation. We resist temptation in thought. We resist temptation in our words and in what we do.

There are those who do not understand. It is not important to have anyone understand. It is only important to know that we have struggled for many centuries to live as we do. We have been and continue to be persecuted in this land of the free by a well meaning people who feel they can come together to pass laws which truly do have an effect on those who in good conscience cannot follow those laws.

We separate ourselves from society because of what God has us do "Be in the world not of the world", in so many words. Romans 12:2 and John 15:9.

We have for many centuries remained this way. People change, they speak about freedom. They speak about their own freedom and persecute those who do not conform to their way.

Whether we are speaking about how to mark our buggies for the street or how we dispose of waste. We have done these things successfully for many generations, yet some will think they know better.

What I personally find annoying is when some from the public in their cars become inpatient in following my family or me while in the buggy. They want us off the road; sometimes they drive recklessly and run us off the road.

They injure and kill our families. We bury them quietly and we forgive them.

Try to remember we were here approximately three centuries ago, on the same farms and on the same paths which you have paved and taken over.

Again and again when I was in my other business I was reminded as today, 'those who do not learn from history will be forced to relive history' and those same mistakes.

The mistakes and evils man has done to his brother and sister of the past and the mistakes and evils man does to his brother and sister today are separated by one 'man'.

Chapter One

As the turbines of the Black Hawk wind down, the crew chief can be seen sliding open the side door, the copilot steps out and to the front of the helicopter as he looks up at the blades.

Samuel, now with the security guard standing off to the side notices part of the flight crew coming toward him. They are the Pilot, Flight nurse, and medic.

"Are you Mr. Hersberger?" The Pilot asks.

"Yes, I'm Samuel Hersberger."

"I am Lieutenant Colonel Simmons. This is Major Donnelly, our flight nurse; and Specialist Long, our flight medic."

"You are here for my wife," says Samuel.

"Yes sir, where is she? She is supposed to be ready for us," cuts in the flight nurse.

"She is still in the emergency room. I don't know what is taking them so long." informs a subdued Samuel, while speaking to Major Donnelly.

Major Donnelly is irritated, as she takes charge. "Jake, I'm going in for her; can you have this bird ready to fly when I come out?"

The pilot, who was looking directly at Samuel, now diverts his attention, looks at the Major smiles and shakes his head. "Consider it done!" he shouts as he turns towards the helicopter.

"Sergeant!" calls Major Donnelly to the crew chief, above the din of the turbines still winding down. "Can you bring the litter? Sarah get the O$_2$ tank, Ekg monitor, pulse ox and aid bag. Mr. Hersberger, lead the way, show us where your wife is."

As they head up the concrete walkway, the crew chief and medic dressed in flight suits with helmets in place and nurse with flight helmet in hand follow Samuel. They cross the parking lot and into the side of the ER as the crew chief holds open the door. Inside they arrive at the triage station. Speaking to the triage nurse, Michele Donnelly is very clinical and to the point.

"Excuse me I'm Major Donnelly; I'm a critical care nurse with the United States Army. We're here for Mary Hers..." She is cut off.

"Just a minute," interrupts the nurse abruptly, as she is distracted.

"Open the door now!" commands the Major. The nurse pushes the button, which opens the door electrically as she looks at the Army Major disapprovingly.

"Where is your wife Mr. Hersberger, show us the way. Specialist and Sergeant follow Mr. Hersberger and get his wife ready to go! I'll see to the paper work."

As they follow him, Sarah spotting a gurney puts all her equipment on it and motions for the crew chief to put the litter in place with the other equipment. They wheel down to the room where Mary now lies. At that moment Army medic Sarah Long takes charge. Getting out a Blood Pressure cuff and stethoscope she has the crew chief get the litter ready.

"Heh Jim, put everything on the floor except the litter, let's get that opened up. I'm going to get a set of signs and check her pulse ox."

Everything begins to go quickly as she continues, "Jim, write this down. One hundred-forty four over eighty-eight blood pressure...ninety-two pulse...twenty-four respirations...pulse ox ninety-nine. Blood pressure is high, but not too bad. Let's move her first, I'll get some help."

Just at this moment Major Donnelly shows up with an ER nurse, laying her helmet aside she listens to the medic.

"Major I got her signs, they're stable and we're preparing to move her. Jim, if you can roll that side of the bottom sheet as I do, we're going to move her with it. Major if you can get the head and ma'am her feet please, let's do this! Sergeant bunch up the sheet and grab hold and pull it tight under her.

Mr. Hersberger if you can wait outside there, give us a little room sir, thank you. Watch the IV! On my command on three, one... two... three, lift and over." Mary is lifted in one smooth motion to the litter. The medic continues, "Major can you hand me the IV?"

"Do we have an IV pole?" asks the Major.

The medic responds, "No ma'am, I have it." After placing a pillow under Mary's head ever so gently, she then takes the IV bag with tubing and places the IV bag under the small of Mary's back.

"We'll hang it in the bird. I have an electronic B/P cuff in the bag ma'am. If we can get that on her we won't be able to hear in order to take one, nor will it be easy to get a pulse in flight. Is the pulse ox still in place?"

The monitoring equipment is changed over quickly to the portable and placed at Mary's head. The O2 line is disconnected from the wall and placed on the tank, which they positioned between her legs.

"Specialist, set the flow rate at two liters," says the major now taking charge after Mary is stabilized on the liter.

"Yes ma'am," responds the dutiful army medic.

Everything is running smoothly. Staff Sergeant Walkins, the crew chief, now can be seen and heard speaking into his helmeted mouth piece as he presses a button on a radio on his hip. "Colonel, get the blades fired up!"

The sergeant looks straight ahead as he listens to the response "Firing up." Nearing the doors, the whine of the turbines can be heard as the blades engage and the beat of heavy props overtake the whine.

cccccc

"Mary, place the kids in the back seat with seatbelts. Let's get over to the hospital and see what's going on," says Bill, as he gathers the families. Mary places the three kinner who are still crying in the back seat and does the best she can to belt them in. She climbs in the front, between her mom and dad.

Fifteen minutes later they are making their way down behind the hospital toward the emergency room parking lot.

As they get closer they here the unmistakable sound of a helicopter.
"Do you here that? Is something coming in?" asks Bill. Everyone is craning their necks looking up as they come around the corner to the lot.

Spotting the helicopter first Mary say's, "It's military, dad."

"Yep, Army, wonder what they're doing here?" responds Bill, urgently.

Helen who is sitting on the right side as they pass the flight crew to their right shouts. "Bill, there's Samuel!" Just then Bill's cell phone rings as they see Samuel on his Blackberry.

"He must be calling us!" Mary say's excitedly, as she turns around in the seat looking back. The kinner are now stretching looking up. Bill pulls the truck into the parking place getting out of the truck Bill and Mary go to and open the back door and reach in to get the children out.

"Mary, can you get Kathryn from that side?" asks her father.
"Yes sir." Mary responds already at the back seat.

They get all the kinner out and as they head toward the back of the truck. The flight crew with Mary makes their way across the parking lot with Samuel. In a loud voice to talk above the din, Samuel can be seen gesturing toward his kinner.

"Can we stop for just a moment these are our kinner," says Samuel, as the co-pilot can be seen exiting the aircraft and waiting for the litter.

Bill, Helen, Mary and all the kinner look on in astonishment first at Mary, on the litter, then at the Blackhawk helicopter with its blades fully engaged.

They quickly close in on Samuel and the Blackhawk flight crew when Samuel looking at Bill addresses him, "I was just trying to call you, I don't have much time, Mary has suffered a stroke they are not able to fully help her here." He is picking up Rachel and Kathryn at the same time, motioning for Bill to get Caleb, who is quickly picked up. He continues, "We are going to Walter Reed. They are waiting for us there. Kinner your mamm is going to another hospital, these fine folks are going to take care of her there and care for her wunderbaar gut, jah!"

Rachel crying again reaches down.

"Mamm," she cries out.

Michele now with helmet in place reaches out for her, again raising her voice above the din she says to him, "Mr. Hersberger, here let me help!" Reaching over, she takes Rachel from him and speaking softly in her ear quiets her as she says, "Here you go sweetie, say something to your mommy she can here you. Do you want to give her a kiss, go ahead you can."

Rachel leaning down places her small tear soaked lips on her mother's cheeks and kisses her.

"I love you mamm," as she touches her face.

The episode is repeated by both Samuel and Bill as they give the other kinner the same opportunity.

The crew chief cuts in, "Ma'am we have to go!" He is looking toward them as he continues, "You can follow with the children go straight in, follow me."

Moving toward the helicopter the props blow everything around. Young Mary's bonnet now is nearly blown from her head, as she grabs at the cloth ties at the bottom of her chin.

Mary, Samuel's wife, bundled onto an army litter is lifted off the gurney as planned, the crew chief taking the head of the litter followed by the medic at her feet. The flight nurse takes the side opposite of the co-pilot. The litter is slid into the litter pan. The crew chief places hearing protection on Mary.

Meanwhile, Samuel is calling loudly toward the children that he loves them and will be back soon. He also reassures them that they will see their mamm again soon and admonishes them to pray.

Pulling Bill up close with his arm around him and speaking into his ear, he asks that he get his mother for the kinner. Samuel then places his home in his friend Bill's care. He gives a hug to each one of the Kramer's, looks at them one more time as he enters the Helicopter.

Chapter Two

The flight nurse and medic are busy readying Mary for the flight. The IV bag is hung, as well as the monitoring equipment is put in place. The crew chief makes sure that Samuel is strapped in.

Exiting the aircraft for the last time he gets everyone away safely. Running back to the bird he pulls the chucks from its wheels throwing them inside and climbs in sliding the door closed behind him.

Staff Sergeant Walkins with his head out the left opening, looks down, then up at the blades. Samuel can here the conversation in his head set.

"Colonel we're clear." And with that, the Blackhawk helicopter raises six feet off the ground, turns clockwise into the opposite direction from which it came, and with a revving of the turbines, the props becoming deafening, the Blackhawk pitches nose down and very quickly it is in flight banking hard to the left in a southerly direction.

cccccccc

Quietly, the kinner can be heard whimpering in the back seat. Mary and Helen are seated in the back with them each holding one of the girls in their laps, close. Helen with one arm holding Kathryn has another around Caleb pulling him close to her.

"There now, your mamm is going to be fine," soothes Helen. Mary is rocking Rachel, as if she were a baby.

"Mamm is going to be ok, she is, she really is," nurture's Mary, stroking Rachel's hair.

It is a short drive back home, to the Hersberger Ranch. As they enter the drive, they can see John's black pickup truck and two buggies. Ranch hands could be seen caring for the horses, Andrew was one of them.

As they pull to a stop, Jeremiah steps from the house appearing somber, mama followed close behind with Katie holding Samantha. Jeremiah appears to speak for all, nears Bill.

"Bill, what is happening? We heard ambulance sirens, John came for us, and he saw the ambulance leave. Please Bill, what has happened, tell me everything, I will not judge, just tell us what is going on," pleads Jeremiah.

"It's Mary, she suffered a stroke," begins Bill.

"We must go there, be with them," cuts in Samuel's mother sharply.

"You can't, she is no longer at the local hospital," continues Bill, understandingly. He looks up at her and into her eyes.

With tears in her eyes, Katie questions, "Where is she?" her voice breaking.

"Apparently, there are complications....." Mama begins to sob, as Katie holds her. Jeremiah, places his right hand on Bill's shoulder.

"Continue, Bill," says Jeremiah, speaking softly.

"They could have treated her there with medication to reverse the stroke, but they are not sure of the effects of the medication on the baby. When we arrived they were moving her to another hospital." Bill now hesitates, looking over everybody.

"Where did they take her Bill, please?" continues Jeremiah, imploring.

"Samuel has arranged for her to be moved to Walter Reed Army Medical Center in Washington D.C." there is stunned silence. Everyone looks at Bill in disbelief.

Then uncharacteristically Jeremiah asks, "This is a good hospital, Bill?"

"The best, he must know somebody important, they sent a helicopter with a full medical crew. They should be arriving their shortly. They were very kind to Mary and the children. I'm sure she is in the best hands."

Silence falls upon the sometimes quietly crying family.

Jeremiah continuing, "Samuel is a gut man, he cares for his family well. This is for our family to pray and to keep close to our hearts. Bill, did Samuel say anything before leaving?" questions Jeremiah now breaking the silence further.

"To notify you, and ask his mother to stay with the children. He asked that I care for his home and the ranch. Is this ok with you, Jeremiah?"

"Yes, I respect his decision and support him as I can. Thank you Bill, Samuel is blessed to have you and your family here."

While the men were talking, Daniel had come from the barn and came up behind Mary. Taking Rachel, who was now sleeping, he comforted her.

Mamma in deep thought can be seen making plans. She begins to bring some order as she instructs, "let us take the children into the front room, so they may sleep close by. It will be dark soon; we should start something to eat. I will also need my things from home."

"Jah, mamma, John..." knowing what is needed, John cuts in.

"I'll take Andrew and Katie with Samantha home and bring back your mother's things, Jeremiah. Anything I can do to help. Please, if you here from Samuel, let me know. Thank You."

"Yes, I will John." The children were placed on the sofas in the front room. Mean while John can be seen driving Andrew, Kate, and Samantha home. He later, after picking up Rebecca's things, can be seen returning.

Jeremiah remained with his family as Daniel spent time with Mary. Helen also remained with Rebecca to help out in the kitchen preparing an early supper.

Bill went for Mr. Schrock, to bring him back to the ranch and explain what happened.

ccccccc

The Blackhawk, flying through bright blue cold skies and carrying Mary, Samuel and the flight crew leave the airspace over Pennsylvania. The flight nurse, Major Donnelly and medic, Specialist Long continue to tend to their patient, as Mary's Husband looks on.

Lieutenant Colonel Simmons can be heard cutting in on the head set as everyone momentarily looks up.

"Mr. Hersberger, do you remember me?" he asks.

Pausing for a moment, Samuel looking forward over his wife, takes in the tone and inflection of the pilot's voice and answers,

"Jah, I remember you. It was Charleston, nineteen seventy-nine. Yes, you were a knob..."

Samuel is stopped mid sentence.

"You gave me a lift back to school, got me past the guards after I signed in late from leave. I'll never forget that. I recognized you from the moment I seen you at the hospital. We'll get your wife into Walter Reed, sir, she'll be fine. I'm not a very religious person, but I see God's fingerprints all over this mission. I know she'll be fine."

"Thank you, Colonel Simmons; you've done well in your life, yes, very gut. Thank you" Samuel stares straight ahead. Then looking down at his wife, he feels God's presence with him and his wife and knows in his heart and soul that yes, his Mary will be fine.

Chapter Three

"Washington Center, Army Helo, Romeo-Tango-Whiskey-Four-Niner-eight," can now be heard as Lieutenant Colonel Simmons is speaking into his headsets mike.

"Army Helo, Romeo-Tango-Whiskey-four-niner-eight, Washington Center, go ahead," responds Washington's air traffic control center.

"Washington Center, Army Helo, Romeo-Tango-Whiskey-four-niner-eight, VFR en route, Walter Reed Army Medical Center, one-thousand feet, advisories, expedite."

"Army helo, Romeo-Tango-Whiskey-four-niner-eight, ident, four-two-seven-niner."
Colonel Simmons punches the code into the Blackhawk's transponder.

Washington Center responds, "Army helo-Romeo-Tango-Whiskey-four-niner-eight, radar contact seven-five miles north-east of Walter Reed, maintain VFR. Advise, any altitude change, stand by for advisories."

As the medevac carrying Mary nears its destination at Walter Reed Army Medical Center, Samuel looking down at his beloved begins to study her being.

Each breath she takes is now matched by his breathing. As she lies quietly, there is a movement of her belly as their baby kicks and moves within its protected womb.

Samuel smiles and a tear traces his face, he traces her figure with his mind's eye. He follows every line of her body to her face, noticing her tiny freckle below her left eye; he remembers the many times he had kissed that very spot.

He sees no pain in her face. Her forehead is without lines. He continues to trace her features to her lips, remembering the first time he touched them with his own.

He remembers the warm moistness and afterward, the look of her eyes as they looked into his, studying his very soul.

Taking his left hand, he runs it over the roughness of his bearded face, he pictures a time not so long ago when she ran her fingers through that same roughness.

He remembers the first time after they were married, the night they shared their physical beings. Their breathing was one, then, also.

Thinking back....*The delicate touch of your hand upon mine... As music floats through us into space.... I look softly into your eyes.... And feel the stroke of your tender cries.... as our touch turns into a warm embrace... Music transforming itself into our feelings... A gentle breeze gives its cue... Our minds, gently as one.... We walk hand in hand through green forests painted crimson....And as the beauty fills us, I have tender thoughts of you.....I love you, Mary.*

Samuel's thoughts are again interrupted by the chatter over his headset.

"Washington Center, Army helo, Romeo-Tango-Whiskey-four-niner-eight, descending to five-zero-zero feet. Have visual, Walter Reed."

"Army helo-Romeo-Tango-Whiskey-four-niner-eight, Washington Center, we have Walter Reed at your one o'clock at five miles, no other aircraft in your vicinity. Radar services terminated. Have a nice day Army."

"Thank You, Washington Center, Army Helo out." The Army Blackhawk medevac, carrying its precious cargo, closes on the helipad at the medical center quickly.

Samuel looking out the side can see an ambulance waiting near the landing zone below him.

Warmly dressed hospital personnel stand at the ready, near the back of the ambulance. He also observes the whiteness of snow on the ground in the surrounding area.

Samuel is awoken from what felt like a dream state from the frigidness of the Washington air. He turns his head to the left toward the voice now just inches from his face.

Willard N. Carpenter

"Mr. Hersberger! Mr. Hersberger! I'm Colonel Connors, hospital commander here at Walter Reed. Mr. Hutchins called and notified us that you were arriving sir. This is Capt. Knight, Deputy Chief of chaplains. He is going to spend the day with you sir. He will have direct access to me if you have any needs we can deal with. Mr. Hutchins will be arriving from Fort Bragg this evening, sir. He will see you here at the hospital. He will give you a call when he arrives to link up with you."

Samuel steps down from the Black Hawk, as they begin the process of moving his wife. Major Donnelly who is very attentive of Mary with Specialist Long looks out at Samuel smiles, and yells, just above the din of the turbines whining down.

"She is doing fine! I suspect you will be a dad again soon."

A very tired Samuel looks and smiles and simply responds, "Yes."

"Mr. Hersberger, your wife is going to be fine, I just know it," she continues.

Lieutenant Colonel Simmons now has made his way to his side of the aircraft and watches as Mary is lifted out. Taking Samuel's hand he says, "I have to return to Indian Town Gap, but I'll be in touch sir, it was good seeing you again, and take care of yourself."

"Yes, danki, and you also Colonel." Lieutenant Colonel Simmons turns toward his co-pilot still seated in the Black Hawk with the door open. While he speaks he is zipping up his flight jacket.

Mary is out of the medevac and now in the ambulance. Samuel is shown the side door of the back of the ambulance, by an army medic. Following close behind is the chaplain.

The ambulance drives away very quickly leaving the flight crew behind. Arriving at the emergency room entrance they are met again.

The door to the ambulance is opened, and standing in the cold, in her green Class A uniform with lab coat is a doctor.

"Mr. Hersberger?" She pauses as the ambulance crew; with the emergency room crew begin to take Mary out of the ambulance. She steps aside making eye contact with Samuel.

"Mr. Hersberger, I am Colonel Corrigan, I am chief of neurology here at Walter Reed, I will personally be seeing to your wife's care."

She reaches and shakes his hand. "Right now she has an appointment with the OB GYN department. We are going to make sure your baby is doing well. Afterwards I will consult with the obstetrician and pediatrician to see how we want to proceed. Do you have any questions sir?"

"Yes, will you be delivering the baby right away?"

"No sir, not necessarily, we want to quickly review everything."

She is interrupted by the Army specialist holding a packet.

"Ma'am this is her records that were given to me. There is an MRI CD ROM also."

"Thank you. Let's go inside, we can wait at the nurses' station up on the OB floor."

Everyone moves through the electronic sliding doors. They make their way to a bank of elevators; push the button on the wall.

Two Army medics stand at either side of Mary's litter. At the back of the elevator is the chaplain. Samuel is standing in front of him and the neurologist is next to Samuel.

Samuel, looking down at his wife, thinks to himself, *Mary, it is moving all very fast. A short time ago we were in our kitchen, speaking, you and I. We were so happy....so happy....The kinner miss you liebe....you must get well...you just must...*

As he wipes more tears from his own eyes, with his right hand he smoothes Mary's hair with his left, tracing her face. He places his hand on her belly.

The baby is motionless. He lingers just as the elevator doors open. They exit and walk down the hallway.

"Mr. Hersberger, follow me please." Mary is taken to a room. A nurse on the floor follows the trio into the room as they are met by another doctor in a lab coat.

"Mr. Hersberger, hi I'm Dr. Hirsh, I'm the obstetrician who will be caring for your wife, right now I'm going to look in on her and we can talk later."

Chapter Four

Walking off, he is met by a nurse coming urgently out of Mary's room. Meeting the doctor she quickly turns back as she is talking,

"Doctor, she's in labor, the baby is crowning!"

"Get her to delivery, stat!" This sets off a flurry of ensuing activity.

"Dr. Nelson to delivery stat!" can be heard over the speaker system. A nurse comes to them and ushers Samuel to a waiting area, along with the chaplain and Dr. Corrigan.

The double doors open, another doctor in scrubs and lab coat enters briskly, briefly looking down then up and ahead. A strained and concerned look pasted to his face.

"Mr. Hersberger that was the pediatrician, apparently we may not have to make decisions regarding whether or not to take the baby. She is doing that for us."

With those words and another nurse is whisking an incubator into the delivery room. The double doors burst open again, with yet another nurse in scrubs pulling on a mask. Hooked behind her ears she tugs the strings to the top of her head.

A second doctor holding a stethoscope walks quickly down the hallway and into the delivery room.

"That was Major Kelley, the chief nurse of the neonatal intensive care unit, along with Colonel Stevens, chief of Pediatrics. Well, sir you have the best in there with your wife. You can be sure of that."

As soon as Dr. Corrigan finishes talking, her beeper goes off. Looking down she shakes her head.

"They are in such a state they didn't know I was out here. I'll be right back."

While pushing the button on her beeper, she makes her way out of the waiting area, walking quickly towards the delivery room; she gives a brief and comforting smile to Samuel as he lowers his head.

At the same time, Major Kelley and Colonel Stevens along with Dr. Nelson rush with the incubator from the delivery room down the hall past Samuel.

Major Kelley gives a small hint of a smile, nodding her head. Then as quickly as they appeared, they are through the double doors and gone.

An OB nurse leaves the delivery room and appears at the door of the waiting room. At first she is somber. Then upon making eye contact with Samuel, she smiles.

"Are you Mr. Hersberger?"

"Jah, I am. How is my boppli and fraa?"

"Sir, I am sorry I don't understand?"

"I'm sorry, my baby and wife."

"You have a son, sir, he is small, five pounds, but he is healthy. He is premature and is being taken to the neonatal intensive care unit down the hall. Your wife is stable there are no complications from the delivery. She is being readied and Dr. Corrigan is having her moved to the medical intensive care unit. Do you have any questions?"

"Thank you, nurse, and no thank you"

Samuel, collapsing onto the sofa breaks down in tears. The chaplain follows close behind placing his hand on his shoulder.

The nurse drops down to the sofa and takes Samuel's hand. Whispering, she moves her mouth to his ear.

"Mary is in good hands Samuel; that is your name?" She leans over in front of him and looks up into his eyes. "They are both fine. I will keep them in prayer. Jesus is here, and he is definitely in charge today."

"Amen!" says the chaplain, seated to the other side of Samuel. "I couldn't have said that better myself."

"Lord, have mercy on me; I have not taken the time to pray. Not once," states Samuel, in exhaustion, staring straight ahead.

"Samuel, the Lord knows your heart, and the prayers of your soul. That is something much deeper and much clearer than your mind can ever produce. Our savior knows our prayers." And with another patting of Samuel's hand she stands.

"Mr. Hersberger, we're headed over to the intensive care unit. Let's get that tPA (tissue Plasminogen activator) into her, ok?" smiles Colonel Corrigan. She is standing square in the door as Mary can be seen past her being rolled by.

Samuel stands quickly; runs a hand over his bearded face, then up through and over his hair, he tracts his wife as she passes.

"Yes, thank you." With a nurse and medic moving Mary on a gurney, they move with purpose through the hallway to the elevator.

Arriving at the unit, the bag of tPA is hung and the infusion begins. Samuel is seated in another waiting room with his new friend from the Chaplains department.

cccccccc

"Colonel Connors, this is Mr. Hutchens. My wife and I are in the lobby. How are Mr. Hersberger and his wife?"

"Sir, good evening, I'll be right there," says Colonel Connor.

Chris Hutchins ends his cell phone conversation, as he looks up a smartly dressed

Colonel Connors in dress greens, comes from around a corner and a hallway.

"Sir, Mrs. Hutchins, how are the both of you this evening?"

"We're fine, Colonel, how are you? And how are the Hersberger's?"

"Mr. Hersberger, I understand is emotionally distraught, understandably so. Mary Hersberger delivered a healthy five pound baby boy. She's been moved to Medical Intensive Care Unit. If you follow me sir, I'll accompany you and Mrs. Hutchins to the unit."

"Thank You, Colonel. We appreciate it."

"You and the Hersberger's are pretty close?" The Colonel begins to make small talk as they make their way to the bank of elevators.

"We go back a ways yes, we just met Mary this past summer when they married."

"They were just married? What a shame, some things just don't seem to be right." Entering the elevator, they ride the short distance to the floor.

Chapter Five

The silver of the elevator doors parting reveals Chris Hutchins with cell phone in hand answering on the first ring.

"Yes, yes, it is a four bedroom house, good, good, and the name? Hersberger, Samuel Hersberger, rank? We'll just call him Mr. Hersberger. My name? Hutchins, Lieutenant General, Hutchins. Assigned? Need to know. Will there be anything else you need? No? Thank You, Thank you very much."

Ending the phone call on his blackberry, Chris with his wife and the hospital commander make their way into the waiting area of the MICU.

The General, spotting Samuel right away, places his hand on his shoulder. Samuel reaches out his hand automatically as he stands.

"Sam, hi! We got here as quickly as possible. How is Mary?"

"Chris thanks for coming, hello Carol." Smiling, Carol approaches in small steps.

Looking around and smoothing her hair back, she gives Samuel a hug. "How are you holding up? Have you eaten?"

"No, not much of an appetite," responds Samuel stepping back and meeting Carol's eyes.

"Yes I understand, but Samuel, your wife and child needs you healthy, Chris you should take these two men down to the cafeteria and get them something to eat. I'll stay here. Let the staff know that I'm here."

"Good idea Carol. Capt, will you join us? Come on Sam let's get you something to eat. What time is it anyhow?" asks General Hutchins, as he is looking down at his watch he continues, "Seventeen-thirty. Colonel, have you eaten yet?"

"No sir, I'll have something brought to the conference room, we can eat there."

"That's great, let's do that, thank you colonel." As they approach the elevators Colonel Connors makes a call on his cell.

Ending his call he informs General Hutchins, "The cafeteria will have dinner for five within a half an hour."

"Six?" Questions Chris Hutchins.

"Yes sir, having a tray sent to your wife in the waiting room," responds the hospital commander.

"Thank You Colonel, very thoughtful."

Settling into the conference room, they are met by personnel from admissions. Samuel shows them his ID card, after it is requested.

Looking at Samuel they inform him, "Sir, we will have to make an ID for your wife also."

"Yes of course, whatever I can do to help facilitate this let me know."

"While you are at it, Samuel, I took the liberty of securing a house for you. I am absolutely certain you will want your family down here with you."

Samuel stares, momentarily before responding, "Yes, thank you Chris."

Chris continues. "Specialist, there will be three other children for Id cards also. This family is Amish; they have a religious objection to their pictures being taken. Can you handle this?"

"Yes sir, may I have the names of all the children?" Samuel lists all the names for the army specialist. The army specialist then finishes with Samuel,

"Thank you sir, Mr. Hersberger, I hope your wife gets well quick. General, Colonel, have a good evening. I'll have this done by tomorrow."

Colonel Connors interrupts the specialist, "When you are done with all those bring them by my office. Ok?"

"Yes sir." Coffee is brought in, as well as hot tea. The Colonel interrupts the wait staff. "Wait just a moment, will you? Gentleman would you care for anything else to drink?" The three men all answer with no, no thank you.

"Coffee is good for me," states the chaplain.

"Sam, have you been to see the baby?"
Chris Hutchins continues.

"Yes, we had just come from there, when
you arrived."

"The baby is healthy," continues the
chaplain. "They are going to keep him there for
a couple of days just to keep an eye on him."

"Good, good. This is good. Samuel there
is housing as I was telling you. Would you like
for me to send someone for your children?"

"No thank you, Chris. I have good friends
who can bring them down."

"Ok, if you need anything else, you let
me know."

A light rattle of metal and plates can be
heard making its way down the hallway as
dinner arrives on a cart by staff from the
hospital cafeteria.

Chicken cordon bleu was on the menu
for that day, along with green beans and
mashed potatoes and gravy, a dinner roll was
in a waxed paper bag. An aluminum pitcher of
ice water was also sent.

The chaplain besides saying grace raised
Mary and the new baby up in prayer also. The
Gentleman began to speak as they ate.

cccccccc

A swish of pants moving quickly brought
a young kitchen staff into the waiting area,

"Ma'am, Colonel Connors asked us to send dinner up to you. There is coffee and ice water. Will you like anything else?"

"No, this was quite nice of y'all and the colonel. Thank you very much." Mrs. Hutchins looks up and smiles.

"Don't mention it, ma'am."

As she begins to eat, a straight faced Colonel Corrigan, steps into the waiting area and finds Mrs. Hutchins with fork and knife in hand as she interrupts, "Mrs. Hutchins, Hi, I'm Dr. Corrigan; I understand you are here for Mr. Hersberger while he grabs something to eat?"

"Yes, I am doctor, any late word?"

"No, only it will be 24 hours until we know anything."

"Give me a minute to inhale this and we can walk down together to the conference room."

"Sure, take your time, Mrs. Hersberger is resting comfortably, and being watched closely."

Mrs. Hutchins finishes her meal then stands, as Dr. Connelly after standing steps back putting out her hand allowing Mrs. Hutchins to walk in front of her.

cccccccc

Samuel with a little perspiration on his forehead stares out the window at the distant

Washington city skyline. He appears a little distant inside the conference room, when he is engaged by a very caring General Hutchins,

"Sam, you know if it can be done anywhere it will be done here!"

His attention Adverted, from the blankness of the dead space that he had created in front of him, Samuel responds to his friend, "Yes, I know."

He shows a hint of a smile as the door opens to the conference room. Mrs. Hutchens, smiling is followed by Dr. Corrigan.

"Mr. Hersberger, I would like to speak with you, would you like to speak in private? Or, I can speak with everyone here."

Samuel, pausing for just a moment, is attentive and answers with authority. "You may speak with all of us."

The doctor pulling a chair sits across from Samuel. At the same time while pulling a chair, Mrs. Hutchins joins her husband.

"Mr. Hersberger, the tPA has been hung and is running. It will be a good 24 hours before we will know anything, if we know anything at all. It will depend on your wife and how quickly she comes to. Then we can see what residuals there might be."

Mrs. Hutchins interrupts, "What do you mean doctor, residuals?"

The doctor looking now at the generals wife, answers, "residuals, would be like not being able to speak maybe some visual problems, but in Mrs. Hersberger's case, and this is what I wanted to bring up, the test, the MRI they had done at Cherry tree hospital showed that the stroke occurred in the cerebellum area of the brain."

Colonel Corrigan is cupping the back of her own head to indicate the area of the stroke.

"It is the size of a small walnut. This area effects balance in walking. The reason I feel that she is unconscious is because of the stress of being pregnant and whatever else she may have been dealing with. We hope to know sometime tomorrow where she is."

Everyone looks around at each other and ends with looking patiently at Samuel.

"Do you or any of you have any questions?" Colonel Corrigan looks from Samuel to the entire group.

With that Colonel Connors stands up, "Well if there are no questions, I think what we should do is see that new born, any thought to a name yet Mr. Hersberger?"

Samuel, taken by surprise looks at the hospital commander for a moment, before responding, "Completely slipped my mind, huh, it completely slipped my mind, hmm imagine." He thinks for a moment.

"Mary and I, we have spoken about names, I will have to sleep on it." They all move towards the door.

cccccccc

Arriving at the viewing area, they all find standing room at the viewing window; a nurse dressed in a yellow scrub dress comes to the window. As everyone is looking for the Hersberger baby, Samuel finds him right away.

The tiny baby still in the incubator with blue name tag is wheeled to the window. The nurse reaches in and first holds up the baby then adjusts him, propping him with a small baby blanket rolled, behind him.

Mrs. Hutchins can be heard aahing the small sleeping figure, bundled against the chill of what could be an otherwise cold world, but not in this corridor, not this night.

For one moment, there was the peace of God. For one moment, one of his miracles lie sleeping peacefully and his mother lay being cared for by a loving and caring staff.

Samuel was amongst those who equally were as cared for as any could be in a family.

Chapter Six

Footsteps, deep in the settled snow are left in pairs of two. Ungloved hands entwined, fingers enmeshed, warmth which makes its way up craved lover's arms.

They stop at their spot right inside the gray woods edge; look around briefly before their eyes meet and as if on cue, drawn to each other, their eyes close and lips come together in passion.

Young Mary without words takes her hands and cradles Daniels face. She leans back briefly, and with her own meets his lips again. Mouth opening slightly she presses into her future, her dreams.

She is placed at arm's length as Daniel now gazes at his warmth in his sight as the sun sets a shimmer in her auburn hair. Her blue gray eyes glisten, as he looks beyond the color and again into her soul.

They speak volumes as generations before may have stood in the very spot as generations before made promises without words from the same place in white snow under a promised lover's feet.

His hands trace his dream of a many time of deep slept nights, tracing her arms at its shoulders, down to her elbows. Leaving go he envelopes her and again draws her near as her arms make their way around his neck and again they come together in moist warmth first of lips, then their faces side by side.

They each slowly feel each other, the moistness of their eyes come together.

"I dream of the night we may feel each other's warmth through the night Daniel. Where we don't have to find a place of our own, out here, where we may find comfort of our own in each other, in our own home, in our own time, in our own place," whispers Mary as she turns her lips to his ear and continues, "I long to have your baby..."

Daniel speechless, looks into Mary's eyes deeply and again kisses her lips as deeply.

"I love you Mary. Ach! We really must leave."

Mary giggles, shaking her head, "or we won't be able to!" She looks again with twinkling eyes at her future, dressed warmly against the back ground of gray and white, bathed in its own cold.

Their hands warm as they again come together, again entwined, again the same feelings surge through them.

Footsteps appear behind them as they walk through the woods between the two properties.

"This is our spot Daniel, it shall always be. We should have our home here."

As if a fire fly flash had gone off in his head quickly and capturing a moment in his own time.

"Jah, I shall speak to my father and uncle! Gut idea!" Daniel's eyes are bright and alive, excited from what he just heard.

They stop turn and look around, then at each other smiling. Mary giggles and they both shake their heads. Mary continues to giggle.

"I have gut ideas also, Jah?"

"We are gut together, Mary. Verra gut!"

As they walk he turns and smiles tenderly at his promised future, with her warm black bonnet and wisps of auburn hair teasing as they hang down the side of her face.

The sun is high and beyond the reach of some white clouds scattered in front of the blueness.

No cold is felt between to unrealized lovers with dreams captured this day in the brightness of bright blues, grays, whites and the beauty of yellow which looks down upon them from afar.

Their dream with a loving God making the plans cannot be matched, touched, dismalled in anyway.

They walk the path that their uncle walked realizing without knowing what he had done not so long ago. How good God is in their savior Jesus Christ. He does care for all.

Making their way through the wood, they come across a fallen tree, Daniel crosses then without warning he reaches under Mary's arms lifting her very powerfully up and across.

As she comes back to rest, crunching upon the snow with twigs under her feet, her hands upon his arms, they stop.

Looking at each other, his hands rest with hers frozen in place. Any excuse to touch each other is grasped, her softness, his warmth, their togetherness.

Breaking through the other side of the woods edge, Daniel's family farm comes into view, as he looks from the farm, to Mary, then back to the farm.

White covered furrows peek above the snow covered open space of a past tobacco field.

A squirrel uncharacteristically is out amongst the trees behind them making some noise amongst the branches. Hearing the noise they bring their heads around together.

A bird chirps out of place for the time of year, its wings flutter, and then the red breast can be seen taking flight.

A physical longing exists with the two young Amish youth, tempered by the reality of Gods plan in their life.

Daniel, still on his Rumspringa, plans to baptize into his faith. Mary, with her continued transformation into what will be her husband's faith and culture, embraces her new life.

But still the longing exists.

"Mary I would like....verra much," carefully Daniel speaks of that longing, "for you to have our boppli....for us to....make"

"I understand Dan...." She pushes her body into his against a tree out of site of the farm below them, at the woods edge; she presses herself into him kissing her Daniel, first on his lips then his face then his neck.

She comes back to his lips again mouth ever so slightly opened.

He feels her softness even through the heavy clothes, though they block out the cold they do not block out the heat of their young passion. They do not stop this time, allowing the physical to continue.

Daniel pushes Mary back and around toward the tree and continues to press this time against her, he presses his mouth to the nape of her neck, kissing her continually as Mary's breathing deepens with his. Her hands around his neck and head she pulls him in tight.

No words whispered or otherwise, leave the lips of the two, unbridled in their passion.

The dance of mouths around necks and hands cautiously searching for a place to shyly explore remains....

Mary's breathing turns from heavy to whimpers....

"Daniel, no, no, we must..."

"Jah, we must stop," Daniel finishes her sentence, kissing her one more time, "Jah...."

Looking at each other they embrace and just hold each other. Though the passion is no longer unbridled, the warmth remains. And there they remained, leaning against the tree, with time passing, holding each other holding each other's future, holding unto the promise of rekindling the passion in a time soon come.

Chapter Seven

Mammmmm!!! Mammmmmmm!!! Caleb, get my phone off my desk! Rachel, go get Mr. Kramer! She collapsed, she is breathing but she is not responsive! I called an ambulance! I'll go out to the road to flag them down.

"Samuel, Sam, heh Sam, wake up!" Chris is standing over Sam as he sits in a chair next to his Mary's bed, his head, wet with perspiration he lays next to her hand. His fingers are just touching hers. Samuel's sandy blond beard and hair are disheveled, with strands here and there.

Mary lay motionless with her head slightly elevated from the bed being cranked up a bit. Her head lies on a pillow white and pure. She lies peaceful, as though visiting for a short time a distant God, but for a short time.

"Sam, been here all night I see, come on let's get some breakfast." Sam looks up at his friend, as he wakes up from his nightmare.

"Morning Chris, breakfast sounds good. I need some coffee."

cccccccc

"Coffee is good. Chris, is that offer to have my kinner brought down still good?" asks Samuel looking at his friend through half open eyes.

"Absolutely, what do you have in mind?" Samuel has got his old friends attention.

"It's Monday, and a bad time to have folks going out of their way to come down here."

Responding, Chris offers, "We can have Tom bring them down Sam, if you like. They know him, or at least they have seen him around."

"That'll be good, yes," says Samuel, thoughtful.

Plans are finalized for Tom to drive back and pick up the children with clothing enough for a couple of weeks.

While at the table at the army hospitals cafeteria, Chris is on the phone, tablet of paper in front of him. The hospitals army chaplain carrying a tray of his own is seen walking over. The tray of food is crowded with a coffee in one corner and a small white bible in the opposite.

Samuel looks over his shoulder to see Colonel Corrigan, Mary's neurologist. Dressed in her dress greens a lab coat draped over her left arm she is entering the cafeteria. She gestures with a smile over to Samuel, "I'll be right there."

Soon all the same people are sitting around the round table talking. While sitting, Mary's doctor begins, "Mary had a good night, and I just came from the floor."

Samuel looks at the doctor and smiles, "I want to talk to her, I just don't know how I'm going to explain all of this."

Chris interrupts, "tell her the truth, Sam. That is what you are good at, just tell her the truth."

"How much of it though," continues Samuel.

"You'll figure that out as you go," responds Chris again.

Everyone, Colonel Corrigan, the army chaplain and Chris are looking at Samuel.

Chris continues while picking up his coffee, "Anyhow, your children will be here by close of day today." He smiles again at his friend.

"Mr. Hersberger, how many children do you have?" asks the doctor.

With a broad smile Samuel responds, "four now." Then as quickly as the smile came, it left, as Samuel left the table mentally, momentarily, he was back on a horse ranch. He was on horseback with his hair drawn back by the wind under his Stetson, and then he is back and the smile returns.

"Ten months ago, I was a bachelor without any children. Now I have four. God certainly had plans for me! I just wish I knew what his plans were going forward."

"Don't we all," says the chaplain. "Well Sam, how about I look into your housing and you go back to your wife. If you need me call me. I believe Tom is already on his way to Pennsylvania.

ccccccc

The nurse is running a warm damp white cloth across Mary's face, as she begins Mary's am care. Mary's hair hangs down the side of her face in a very long pony tail. Strands stick to the new dampness high on her cheek, moved with each tender stroke of the wash cloth.

She looks peaceful as she sleeps into the beginning of her second day. A sheet lies over her; a hint of a hospital gown is seen through the sheet in paisley. A basin of warm water with soap next to it was on the over head table. The fragrance of soap and lilacs wafts the room.

As the nurse gently takes Mary's arm and hand in her own to wash it, there is a little movement, a twitch perhaps, voluntary or involuntary?

Young First Lieutenant Carver, stopping looks and takes Mary by the hand and felt a slow closing of fingers over her own. She next notices Mary move her head to one side, as she breathes out heavily.

"Mrs. Hersberger...Mary...Mary...can you hear me? Squeeze my fingers with your hand." Mary ever so lightly clasps her hand around Lieutenant Carver's fingers, and then begins to squeeze a little tighter.

Jessica reaching over takes hold of the nurse call button with a smile. Within a moment the charge nurse, Capt Elizabeth Wills was in the room looking at the Lieutenant smiling then down at a more responsive Mary Hersberger.

"Look at that, I'll page Doctor Corrigan." Giving another smile she leaves the room and picks up the phone.

ccccccc

Looking down at her belt with the beeper, Colonel Corrigan gives a concerned look as she is standing outside of the elevator. The doors opens and Samuel, the chaplain Captain Knight and the Colonel walk on, the door closes while the doctor pushes the button.

A short time later those silver doors open and Colonel Corrigan with a little more purpose to her step walks quickly through the unit's doors being met by the charge nurse still holding a smile.

"Relax; Mrs. Hersberger is beginning to respond. Jessica is in doing her bed bath now. You must be Mr. Hersberger? Hi, I'm Captain Wills, I'm the charge nurse."

"Hi Captain, my wife, what did you say?" asks Samuel with a hint of hope within his voice.

"The Captain was just telling me that your wife is responsive. Why don't you wait in the waiting room, while I catch up and see what's up," says Mary's doctor, still smiling cautiously.

cccccccc

"Hersberger ranch, Bill Kramer," came the short answer to the phone call.

"Bill, its Sam."

"Sam, how y'all doin down their?" responds an otherwise tired but hopeful ranch manager.

"Apparently Mary is coming to. We have a baby boy, Bill. Can you imagine?"

Congratulations, the big news is.... Mary is beginning to come to?" questions Bill.

"Jah, the doctor is in with her at the moment. The reason I'm calling is because a house has been secured for me down here, while Mary is in the hospital. Tom is on his way up to pick up my kinner.... If someone else wants to come down also to help with the kinner it would be ok and appreciated. It'll be pretty busy. Also I have a trunk on top of my safe, I'll need that."

"When is he expected?" asks Bill.

"Around noon I suspect, he's driving, should be showing up in a black suburban," says Samuel, a little more matter of fact.

"Sam, it's a little light for a Monday, I'll go speak to your mom and get things moving. Maybe I'll have Helen talk to her with me."

As Bill is talking a horse and buggy makes its way, clip clopping down the drive. Looking out from the front of the stables he sees Samuels's mom and another young woman whom he doesn't know. She is Amish, resembling Katie to an extent.

The horse and buggy comes to a halt at the fence used for hitching of horses of the horse and buggies which frequented the Hersberger Ranch. Bill was the first to meet the two women with the three Hersberger children.

"Howdy ladies, Ma'am," greets Bill holding out his hand to Samuel's Mamma. "I just got off the phone with Samuel."

"Ach, how is he doing, how is Mary," asks Rebecca, Samuel's mother.

"Well she is beginning to come to; the doctor is in with her right now. They had a baby boy," pausing Bill awaits a reaction. He didn't wait long when both woman clutched their hand to their chests and looked directly at Bill.

"Ellie, ist diese wunderbare ja. Ich wünschte, wir könnten es gewesen sein," says an excited Rebecca.

Looking at Bill again she continues, "I'm sorry Bill, I am so excited I didn't introduce you, this is one of my granddaughters, Ellie Grau. I was just telling her that the news is wonderful and that I wish we could have been there."

"Good morning Ellie, It's nice to meet you," greets Bill holding out his hand to shake. A little hesitant Ellie holds out her hand receiving Bill's.

"Yes it is good news; it would have been nice for all of us to be near. But the important thing is that Mary sounds as though she will be ok."

"Jah Bill, this is good news."

"The reason I came out here to see you is that Samuel has temporary housing and has sent a car for the children so they may be near to their mother. He also said that if anyone else wanted to come down and help with the children, it would be welcomed." Again Bill pauses as Rebecca now looks at Ellie.

"Ellie had some time; she is here from Ohio to visit, but told me she would like to help. But I don't know about Washington. Ellie what do you think? Möchten Sie mit dem zu Samuels reisen und beobachten Sie die Kinner ihr?" Rebecca looks at Ellie as she responds right away.

"Ja, Ich mag mit dem Kinner reisen. Jah, I will like to travel with the Kinner, Bill. I will do whatever to help." Smiling, Ellie brightens as she looks at Bill. "I am doing a lot of traveling. I arrived by train from Ohio Saturday. Today I travel to Washington, gut!"

cccccccc

"Mr. Hersberger, good morning sir, I'm Lieutenant Carver. I will be your wife's nurse today. I just finished giving your wife her AM care. You can go in now," say's Jessica softly, as she reaches up clutching the stethoscope hanging from around her neck.

Samuel gazes into the drab whiteness of the room without windows. Mary lies quietly, covered with a white cotton blanket cuffed at the top with a white sheet. The center of the blanket is marked with a caduceus and U.S. on either side of it.

Taking a deep breath Samuel with a little perspiration walks into the room and back to where he was not too long ago sleeping.

Chapter Eight

Her hand is warm, as he rests them in his own, running his thumb over the back and paleness of it. His other hand sweeps up and over her forehead, slightly damp as he looks at her closed eyes. They reflect a calmness of heaven.

As he slides his hand down the side of her face Mary slowly turns her head into his hand, "Samuel...mein Samuel...wo bist du?" she asks as she turns her head again, towards her love, sensing his presence his warmth.

"Mary, Mary I'm here meine Liebe," whispers Samuel, again running his hand down the right side of her face. As he does, Mary's eyes open ever so slightly. A glisten appears, peering out at his own tired eyes.

"Samuel, meine liebe," whispers Mary, struggling to speak.

"Yes Mary, I'm here," whispers Samuel, now with a slight smile. Mary stares as if to focus, her eyes shifting side to side, then into Samuels eyes again. Closing them one more time, she opens them with a question, "What happened? Where am I?"

"You collapsed Mary, you had a stroke," says Samuel as he closes on his wife's face with his own. He reaches for the nurse call button. "You are going to be ok though," he continues as he now presses the button.

The two are staring at each other as Lieutenant Carver comes into the room to their side of the bed. "Mrs. Hersberger, well hello there. Look at you! I'm Lieutenant Carver, you can call me Jessica. I'm your nurse."

Mary's eyes dart at the nurse and back at Samuel, then again at the nurse.

"I'm in a hospital," says Mary as she begins to understand what is going on. "My bobbli," she whispers in a panic as she places her hand down onto her belly. Crying she says again "My boppli!"

"Mary, your baby is fine! You have a healthy baby boy," says her nurse as she grasps Mary's hand.

"Mary, you had the baby yesterday which was Sunday," says Samuel.

"Today is not Sunday?" Mary now looks wide eyed at Samuel.

"No, you have been sleeping," adds Jessica and continues. "I'm going to leave now and let your doctor know that we have a very awake Mary Hersberger."

"We have a baby boy Samuel?" a slight smile takes hold on her face, as she looks again into Samuels eyes. Tears stream down not just on Mary's face but also Samuels, leaving trails of reminders of what has become many.

"Jah Liebe," he says with tears melting over his smile...taking her hands in his own he pulls them to his face and holds them close and against the right side of his cheek. God's peace washes over them at this moment.

cccccccc

The black suburban can be seen pulling quietly and slowly down the drive of the Hersberger ranch. Bill inside of the corral next to the driveway walks over to and climbs the three railed fence, hopping over it. He then dusts himself off and removes his gloves while walking over to the more familiar looking vehicle.

Both front doors open at the same time as Tom steps out from the driver seat and a young woman steps out from the passenger side. Both are dressed in business casual clothes.

Tom approaches Bill, "Hello sir, I'm Tom Hastings, this is Susan Bennett. I'm a friend of Samuel's. Susan is his executive officer."

"I'm Bill Kramer, I'm also a friend of Sam's and I manage his ranch. He called me to be expecting you. I spoke to the family, they're also expecting you. Army?" asks Bill as he looks at the young woman.

"I'm a First Lieutenant in the U.S. Army, yes sir. I'll be Mr. Hersberger's aid while he is in Washington. It's nice to meet you." Lieutenant Bennett holds her hand out, shaking Bill's hand.

Grinning Bill says again, "Army."

"Yes sir!" Susan Bennett smiles back, as a squeaky wooden screen door can be heard off to her left side.

Bill looks over at Samuels' mother and his three children can be seen coming out of the house with Ellie Grau walking behind them. As Bill looks over the screen door slams close.

"Rebecca this is Lieu....!"

"Hi I'm Susan Bennett, I'm Mr. Hersberger's aid, I'll be helping you all out while you are in Washington," cuts in the Lieutenant abruptly, while briefly looking at Bill.

"Pardon me sir," she continues.

As Ellie makes her way forward she raises her head making eye contact with Tom.

Tom noticing reaches out with his hand gently.

"Hi, I'm Tom Hastings," he says with some excitement in his voice.

"I know a lot of the family members of Sam's but I don't believe we've met," he continues while still looking at Ellie with a smile.

"Hello Tom, I am his niece, I am packed are we ready to leave?" asks Ellie, the excitement building.

Cutting in, Susan using Ellie's announcement, hastens the departure.

"Yes we are... good idea to get on the road. We can get in before dark and these children can see their mom and dad." They make their way toward the suburban.

"Tom, what do you think about we putting the children in the back seat, have Miss Grau sit up front with you, I'll sit in the jump seat in the back."

"Sounds good, Miss Grau...."

"I'm actually Mrs. Grau, but please call me Ellie," she playfully cuts off Tom still smiling at her.

"Yes ma'am," Tom responds, as he opens the door for her and continuing "you're married?"

"Jah," Ellie puts her head down, and quiets, then raising her head, smiles at Tom again.

"Two years now."

Meanwhile Susan is putting seatbelts on the children.

"You smell nice," say's Rachel with her face in Susan's hair. Susan turns her head quickly, her hair fanning Rachel's face making her giggle and she shakes her head back and forth.

"I do?" questions Susan, now face to face with the little girl, smiling widely. She tosses her hair back behind her. She takes her finger and touches the tip of her nose, "and you are so cute!"

Rachel giggles again, nose wrinkling, when Susan can feel a poking on her arm.

"Am I... am I cute too!" sounds Kathryn, not to be out done. Susan, leans back, and out of the car.

"Oh yes you are, all of the Hersberger children are just beautiful! Yes!"

As she speaks she applies the children's locks inside of the door of the right side.

Walking around to the left side she looks through the windshield at Tom and Ellie still speaking.

"I'm applying the child safety lock on this side, and then I'll get in the back," she says as she passes the driver window.

"Ok Susan, need help?"

"No I have it, thanks anyway." Bill helps with the lone trunk and small amount of luggage.

The back door of the suburban is closed with its precious cargo and is started up.

From Bill's vantage point with Samuel's mother he can see everyone waving.

cccccccc

"Hi, I'm Doctor Corrigan, and you are..."

"Mary Hersberger," says Mary, now looking up at the Doctor. She stands dressed in her dress greens with lab coat.

Over the left pocket is written in red embroidery Colonel M. Corrigan D.O. Then under her name Chief, Neurology.

"Let's see now. Hold my fingers," as she watches Mary raise both of her hands and grasp her fingers of both hands.

"Now squeeze like you holding onto your children to keep them safe."

Mary squeezes very hard, the intensity can be seen in her eyes.

"Where are my kinner," she asks with a strain.

"Leib, they are on their way here," says Samuel lovingly.

"They are coming here? Is Bill bringing them, my father does he know how I am? They should be here in a few minutes if they are on their way...."

"Mary, it will take them a little over three hours to travel here by vehicle. Tom left this morning to pick them up in a car. Your father is being kept informed as to your condition."

Mary stares in confusion.

"Where am I, Samuel?"

After what seemed like a very long pause. Samuel answers slowly, "You are in a hospital in Washington D.C. You were very serious; the doctors at Cherry Tree Hospital could not help you without harming the bobbli.

I called Chris for help; he sent help to move you here."

"But we did not have the complications that we were expecting Mrs. Hersberger. As soon as we got to the OB floor to examine you, you went into labor and delivered a five pound baby boy. Problem solved. I am your neurologist and I moved you to where you are now, the medical intensive care unit. We gave you tPA, which basically opened or cleared your blood vessels in your brain. Apparently it did quite well. Now I need to continue this, Mr. Hersberger if you could step out sir, please."

Samuel steps out of the room after kissing Mary on the forehead, Dr Corrigan continues with the exam.

"Let's see you move your left foot, ok now the right. Good, good! Now stick out your tongue. Open your mouth wide. Pull your right knee up to you, now the other. Without moving your head follow my finger with your eyes. Still, real good Mary, do you mind if I call you Mary?"

"No I don't mind, where am I? What hospital am I in?" asks a very inquisitive Mary.

"You are at Walter Reed Army Medical Center, which is in Washington D.C."

"How am I in this hospital?"

"Your husband must be very important to this country, if you're here Mary."

"Jah, but now, who is Samuel?" asks Mary staring straight ahead.

"I don't know my husband." Looking to the right, out the door towards her husband she reiterates in a whisper, "who are you Samuel Hersberger?"

Chapter Nine

Colonel Corrigan looks at her patient then out the door herself at the lone figure with long blond hair and straggly beard. He looks very tired, his face is pail and gaunt. He stares a thousand miles away, though he was right next to the nurse's station. His eye lids droop, it conceals some of the distance.

"Mr. Hersberger, sir, you may go back in," says the Colonel. She continues to look out at the lone figure. *Yes, who are you Samuel Hersberger?* Wonders Colonel Corrigan while walking to the nursing station.

cccccccc

"You look so tired Samuel, kumme, sit here with me. Let me be with you, look at you." As Samuel sits, Mary reaches for him taking his right hand with her own. His hand is pulled to her face as she kisses his fingers.

"Liebe, what you must have gone through in the past 24 hours." She gently pulls his hand to her chest and embraces it.

"I love you very much, nothing can change that Samuel. I have made promises to God when we were married. Nothing will change that. You are a gut man, daed, and husband. I know this. You have gone through much to save me and our boppli. I know this. Nothing can make me feel more for you, not now, not tomorrow. Samuel, look at me liebe, it is time for you to trust me with your future. It is time for you to rest with me to stop worrying about the unknown. Samuel, who are you?"

Samuel is distraught in his appearance.

"Jah, it is time. I will show you and the kinner who I am, I will do the best I can to tell you what I did and do now. The kinner will be here shortly. I will be back with them and will explain to all of you."

"I want to see my boppli, Samuel, Please," pleads Mary.

cccccccc

"Mrs. Hersberger and her husband will be coming down to see their baby, let's find a room where they can all be together alone."

"Yes maam," responds the young medical specialist. A couple of minutes later the young specialist dressed in his light gray scrubs can be seen rolling the bassinet to a quiet room.

A noise from his right hastens a look to the sound. The door to the department can be seen opening with a nurse pushing Mary in a wheel chair, she is all smiles as she is wheeled through holding Samuels hand.

"Mrs. Hersberger, Mr. Hersberger, well you look well ma'am," smiles the nurse from the newborn nursery. "I'm captain Sheeran, I'm the charge nurse today, if you have any questions please feel free to ask."

"Thank you Captain," responds Samuel while laying his hand on Mary's shoulder. Mary looks up smiling as she lays her hand on Samuel's.

"Your baby was just moved into this room by the specialist. He is still in there." The door is opened and the trio walks through the doors past the bed to the quiet bundle in a light blue blanket on his side.

"Ma'am, I'm specialist Johnson, here is your baby," he stoops over with his six foot frame and gently cradles the tiny baby's head and shoulders with his left hand slowly lifts him out and over to Mary, who is now crying while smiling.

"May I get the two of you anything?" he asks as he makes contact with Mary's hand and arms now resting the baby into the warmth of his mother.

Mary pulls the infant into her bosoms, close. "We have started the baby on bottle formula ma'am; there is uncertainty as far as the medication used to help you versus your breast milk. You will not be able to breast feed."

"I am alive and I am holding my boppli, God is gut."

"Yes ma'am," the specialist smiles down at Mary now looking up at him.

"If you will excuse me I will be in the nursing station if you need anything...sir," the specialist passes them.

"I'll be outside also, you have about fifteen minutes, and then I'll be in to bring you back. Remember you can't be up to long if you feel any cramping or if you have any bleeding come and get me ok?"

"Yes nurse," responds Mary "I feel fine, thank you I will."

cccccccc

"Daed, daed, daed!" could be heard the screams of little voices as they get out of the car and see their father for the first time in 24 hours. Little arms wrap around his legs as he lifts each, one at a time and squeezes them with his strength and warmth.

"Mr. Hersberger, I take it?" Sir...hi...I'm Lt. Bennett. I will be your aide while you're here sir."

"Lieutenant, thank you, Ellie, Bill called and told me your coming, and this is a pleasant surprise. How are you?

"Gut uncle, wie gehts?"

"Gut! I just came from Mary; we were visiting with our boppli. Mary is lying down now; she is excited about seeing the rest of our kinner. This is Captain Knight; he has been a constant source of inspiration here for me as Chaplain here at the hospital."

"Ma'am, it's nice to meet you," Captain Knight holds out his hand to greet the young Amish woman. I understand that there is a mom up there awaiting her young uns would you like to accompany me?"

"Jah, do I call you Captain?"

"No ma'am, if you are comfortable you can call me Reverend Knight. Outside of the Army I would be a Lutheran Pastor. You are Amish yes?

"Yes, we are."

"Would that be Old Order, New Order, or Beachy? Do I have that right?"

"Yes reverend, verra gut, you are well read. We are New Order."

They are going through the doors to the hospital as they keep up the conversation with the three children looking back and forth at them and each other, all the while taking in the surroundings of all the white coats and uniforms.

The enormity of the inside of the building is something they have never seen as can be noticed by little eyes turned very big.

"I studied it on the side while I was at seminary in Gettysburg, Pennsylvania."

"Not too far from us, Reverend Knight."

"I know, I understand you aren't from Lancaster County but to the east in Chester County. Correct?"

"Jah, Honeybrook, Jah! I was born and raised there, now I live in an old order community in Sugar Creek, Ohio. I followed my husband" A little excitement hinting in her voice as she shares with the Army Chaplain.

cccccccc

The children arriving on the unit initially turn up their noses. Off to the left a nurse is wiping down a bed newly emptied with alcohol. The chaplain, Ellie and children are met by Mary's nurse. Little noses turned up are now turned into gazes of worry and wonderment, as they round the corner into their mother's room.

"Mamm!!" is heard the simultaneous screams from all the children.

"Shhh! Sick people here, kinner," says Ellie. Her nurse, watching from off the side, giggles.

"Little ones," she says as she shakes her head no with a grin.

"Rachel, kommen Sie bitte schnell an deine Mamm!" with a big broad smile she runs to her mother bouncing up on the bed! She has no words following as she is followed by Caleb.

"Mamm Ich liebe dich," says Caleb in German.

"I love you too!" Mary beams down pulling his head to her. "I love you verra much also, jah!" Caleb burrows his head into his mother's arms clutching onto her arms with both of his and holding her very tight. A little whimper can be heard.

"You still love me too mamm?" with tears in her eyes and voice. Kathryn looks on in fear. "Especially, kumme Kathryn to your mamm's arms schnell," and with Mary's words Kathryn instantly smiles and jumps on the foot of the bed and climbs up the middle.

"Easy now Kathryn, mamm has had a boppli, slide up to me gently, jah, that's it." Kathryn now lays her head on Mary's Bosom. Kathryn whispers....

"I can hear your heart beat mamm."
"Jah."

ccccccc

"Sir, are you about ready? General Hutchins has arrived and is down stairs,"

First Lieutenant Bennet, a grad of The Citadel has been a United States Army officer for three years. She stands in the upstairs hallway of the new but temporary home of Colonel Samuel Hersberger and his family. He turns from the full length mirror as he rubs his face, towards his aid. "Well sir, you certainly look different without the beard and a haircut." The lieutenant smiles at him and Samuel smiles back.

"Yes, I have to think in English again. Not a problem but I have been through many changes. We have been through many changes. One more, one more change Lieutenant."

"Yes Sir, we'll be with you. They have no idea who you are?"

"They will, very shortly they will," says Samuel with some concern in his face. He looks again at his aide.

"Shall we, lieutenant?"

"Yes sir!"

"General, you haven't waited long I hope."

"Long enough to here you up their admiring yourself, Colonel," laughs Chris, his old friend and superior.

"Looking good, yes sir looking good!"

"How do you feel?"

"Nervous, but confident."

"Let's do this then!"

Chapter Ten

"Maam, I just spotted senior officers coming down the hall with Colonel Corrigan." Captain Wills picks her head up from the desk and stands as she responds to Mary's nurse, Lieutenant Carver.

"Thank you, Jessica." They both walk towards the main doors of the medical intensive care unit. They are met by the chaplain, Captain Knight. Ellie Grau stands in front and just outside of the door of Mary's room.

The nurses can hear the young voices from where they stand when in walks General Hutchinson with Colonel Corrigan, Mary's doctor; Colonel Connor, the hospital commander; and Samuel Hersberger. "General, may I help you?" asks Captain Wills.

"Yes we are here to see Mary Hersberger," states the General matter of factly.

"Mrs. Hersberger has visitors already, they're too many of you...we have already made an exception to allow the children on the unit. Does Mr. Hersberger know that all of you are here?"

With a smile on his face he looks over his right shoulder, "Sam do you know we're here?

"Mr...I mean sir...I beg your pardon. I didn't recognize you," stammers Captain Wills.

"Don't worry about it Captain, seems like a lot of folks are going to have the same problem today."

"Captain, can we see ourselves clear of making several exceptions today? We have Doctor Corrigan here to oversee things." Colonel Connor the hospital commander asks.

"Yes sir," responds the head nurse.

cccccccc

"Mary, many English, soldiers in uniforms coming here to see you," says Ellie from the doorway. The children turn towards the door, and then one by one they leave Mary's side and go outside of the room and with big bright eyes peer down at the congregation of green uniforms some with white lab coats coming toward them.

"Daed?" Caleb can be heard whispering as he recognizes his father dressed differently.

"I think we know our kinner, smiles Samuel as he lifts Rachel giving her a kiss on the forehead. She is blankly staring at him and raises her hand and rubs his face.

"Daed?" she asks confused.

"Jah...daed!" he laughs in response. He sets her down, rustles Caleb's hair then kisses the top of his head, "Sohn," he gently whispers. "Kathryn."

Samuel lifts his daughter up and holds her close as she encircles his neck, "I love you daed," she says.

"I love you too."

"Now that everyone is done loving each other, someone please tell me what is going on out there!" blurts out a feisty Mary.

Stepping in Colonel Corrigan begins, "Hi Mary, it seems an explanation as to what you are doing here and who your husband is, is due. So we are here to tell you everything."

She is smiling down at Mary reclined up in her bed. She continues, "Would you like a little water?"

"No, doctor, I'm fine really." Mary brushes back her hair which dropped down into her eyes.

"Yesterday a little longer than 24 hours ago you suffered a cerebellar embolic stroke, which means a blood clot went to a part of the brain which is responsible for balance. Samuel, your husband was not given many choices in how to save you and your baby's life. He called his...both of you...your friend Chris Hutchinson," begins Colonel Corrigan as she pauses.

"He is a United States Army General." Another pause "He arranged for a Helicopter to move you both to our care. You know what we have done here so far. Now...he will have to tell you the rest."

With that Mary's doctor steps out and stepping in dressed in green uniform Chris Hutchins. He stood tall, holding a green beret, his dress greens had a blue flash of a sword with lightning bolt coursing through it on his left sleeve. Atop of both his shoulders three silver stars in alignment.

"I would like for the children to be in here, when I tell this," Chris Hutchins looks out the door and with his left hand waves them in.

As they enter he begins with picking up Kathryn and placing her on his knee. He is now sitting at the foot of Mary's bed in a straight back chair; he looks to his left and pulls Rachel in close encircling her with his left arm.

He then directs Caleb with his eyes to the opposite side.

Looking directly at Mary he begins.

"You know my name Mary, what you don't know and what you have figured out by now is that I am a part of the United States Army. I am in charge of Special Operations Command. Much of what we do we do at the direction of the President of the United States. All of what we do is secret."

Continuing General Hutchins describes what Samuel did.

"Samuel, your husband is...was in charge of a secret unit within Special Forces known as First Special Forces Operational Detachment-Delta. He is a United States Army officer with the rank of Colonel. He remains with the unit today as an advisor. The unit's mission is that of counter terrorism. Another words he goes after bad people...terrorists. Do you understand Mary; he is a good guy, a remarkable leader. Don't judge him too harshly, ok?"

"I...Chris, I love my husband verra much. It is not for me to judge," speaking softly while looking down, Mary slowly looks over and smiles at Chris Hutchins.

"Colonel Hersberger, you're on!" exclaims the General still looking at Mary as he stands.

Colonel Samuel Hersberger, holding his beret in hand and having a similar appearance to his 'boss' enters the room slowly at first, peeking around the corner. He looks at Chris and shakes his hand, "thank you sir."

Mary can be seen gingerly moving to the right side of the bed and spreading the linen on the left with her hand. "Samuel, meine liebe, kumme."

"Jah," says Samuel, eager to hear any pleasantries from his wife."

"Ellie, nehmt die Kinder weg bitte."

"Captain Knight, please take these cards and take our children with Ellie down stairs to the cafeteria."

"Yes sir," responds the chaplain taking hold of Kathryn's hand. "Are you hungry?"

"I am!" responds Ellie, smiling at the chaplain.

As they leave, Mary begins asking, "Ich fühle ich lerne, die mein Mann ist. Sie sind ein Soldat, jah."

"Jah, I am a soldier, I have been a soldier for twenty years."

"Samuel, du hast das Leben von anderen Menschen genommen?"

After hearing the question of truth of his faith and culture, he stairs and responds forthrightly and honestly, "Jah, I have taken the life of many men," tears well in his eyes, as he breaks eye contact, looking down at the purity of white sheets, with small wrinkles. He nervously spreads them flat as Mary takes his hand tenderly and holds it.

"Sie haben versucht, Ihnen zu nehmen," she looks as though seeing through him, remembering the scar on his back.

"Jah, they have tried to take my life, many times."

"Dein Leben manchmal war sehr hart."

"Jah, my life at time was verra hard."

"Krieg ist schrecklich." Mary looks away, tears are now falling down her face.

"Jah, war is awful, no soldier likes war meine liebe." Samuel, now reliving many awful moments of his past stares past her and begins to openly cry.

"Kumme Samuel, I do not judge you," she reaches quickly for him clasping onto his shoulders, pulling him close.

Samuel openly weeps, relieved by his understanding wife, but mostly discarding many years of those things which went against his teachings.

He weeps, discarding a lifetime of the harsh reality of war, he weeps. This man weeps and tears cleanses his soul and he knew when he left that room he would leave with his wife and life anew.

Colonel Samuel Hersberger weeps and with his crying he stepped out from his father's shadow.

Chapter Eleven

"Colonel Hersberger, good morning sir, we are moving Mary to a Medical floor, we feel she is no longer critical," explains Colonel Corrigan looking at Samuel with a smile. "It's been three days, a lot has happened. I need to speak to the two of you where we go from here."

Colonel Hersberger has chosen to live his life as an army officer for the remainder of his time in Washington D.C. He now openly wears his BDU's (Battle Dress Uniform) He proudly wears his green beret, a silver spread eagle presents on the flash. Black boots are shined to a high gloss finish.

Mary wears sweats, her hair is not pulled up, and it remains braided and hangs down to beyond her waist. U.S. Army is printed big across her chest of the grey sweat shirt.

ccccccc

As they walk into Mary's room she is being assisted by a physical therapy technician. Specialist Brown is assisting her into a wheelchair. "Ma'am, sir good morning we are just about to leave for PT."

"If you could give us a moment specialist, we should all sit." Colonel Corrigan finishes and Specialist Brown volunteers.

"I'll get a couple of more chairs." He returns a moment later with two chairs.

"Specialist sit, please," says Samuel looking up at the young specialist standing by the door.

"Thank you, sir." Specialist Brown makes his way to a chair next to Mary's bed at the head and pulls it towards the rest of the group.

"Mary, let's do an update," begins Dr. Corrigan. "Three days ago you suffered a stroke which affects your balance. You delivered a healthy baby..." There is a light knock on the door. The specialist looks at the doctor who shakes her head at him while he is standing and opens the door. Present is Major Kelly Chief nurse of the neonatal intensive care unit. With her is Colonel Stevens Chief of Pediatrics.

Colonel Corrigan continues, "thanks for coming, this is Major Kelley chief nurse of the neonatal intensive care unit and Colonel Stevens who is chief of Pediatrics."

"Good morning," says Mary in English.

"Good morning," repeats Samuel with a broad smile.

"I'll get a couple of more chairs," says Specialist Brown now looking out at the nursing station, vacated except for one nurse sitting doing paper work.

With all sitting, Mary and Samuel continue to smile broadly.

"As I was saying, it has been three days. Mary your brain is fine. You are about 99%. With therapy you will be back to normal and walking within a few weeks. I have one more concern; I feel the cause of the stroke is related to the patent foramen ovale (PFO). It is a small hole in the heart between the left and right atria, the upper two chambers of your heart. This is new research, and there are procedures to help close this opening. A medical university in Philadelphia holds promise as to helping those with this opening which is left over from infancy. I have been in contact with this doctor and feel that he can help us."

"What does this mean," asks Mary.

"We can do nothing and we can continue to treat you with medications to avoid another stroke, or if we close the opening we can lessen the chances. You will still be on medications for the rest of your life but it will be less medications. I feel this will go a long way in keeping you healthy. There is also a side benefit. We are finding that the PFO also is a cause of some migraines, which you had indicated that you have regularly."

"I do not want a hole in my heart, what do I have to do to get it closed," asks Mary who is still smiling, just a little less. Samuel looks over at her and listens.

"It is as any procedure not easy or simple. They will numb you at your right groin site. Insert a catheter into the artery which has attached to it a device which resembles a double umbrella. They go into the heart, through one side of the foramen, the wall, open the umbrella pull back then open an opposite umbrella and pull it close from the other side. They then pull the catheter out and the hole is closed."

A pause and Mary smiles, "you make this sound easy Doctor."

Doctor Corrigan returns her smile. "It is not easy; a lot of talented people will be at work. What do you think?"

"Jah, I would like this," responds Mary.
"I will see what the doctor who specializes in this, schedule is; I believe you are looking at a trip to Philadelphia Mary." She straightens up with a smile, looking over at the pediatrician.
"Well, it's time for your baby to leave what we need to know is there someone to care for him and we need a name."

Mary looks again lovingly at Samuel. "We knew this was coming we are ready to bring our boppli home. Well, home as we know it now. Ellie is here from her home to help watch our children and the new boppli. Samuel has a name which I also like. Christopher. Jah, Christopher." They look approvingly at each other with slightly misty eyes to add to their smiles.

"Christopher is a gut name," says Samuel approvingly. He looks down momentarily, then up and around the room, "when can he come home?" he asks.

"Now!" says Major Kelley.

Samuel reaches into his pocket pulling out his blackberry, turns it on and lifts it to his ear. "Lieutenant, this is Colonel Hersberger, I need you to escort Mrs. Grau to the hospital. Bring the car seat. We have a baby to bring home." He smiles again while looking around the room.

ccccccc

"Ellie the delivery men are here!" explains Susan, Samuel's aide who now is becoming good friends with Ellie.

"The boppli's things are going in my room. I will be able to care better for him this way." Christopher can be heard fussing from a small basinet, meant for him to sleep temporarily. The brick two story home in Washington is warm with dinner being prepared in the kitchen.

The children play quietly on the living room floor a small board game that was gotten for them by Lieutenant Bennet to help occupy them during the supposed short winter days which have become long for the children.

Chutes and Ladders and Barrel of Monkeys lay out on the floor where they are very quiet playing with each other

Every so often Kathryn will look up at Caleb and smile. Wisps of her blond hair hang down in her face. She blows them with pursed lips.

Rachel giggles at how she continues to blow the hair out of her face but not physically move them. She then gently moves it to under her kapp.

"Here Kathryn, let me fix this." Kathryn looks to her right at her sister.

The quiet is broken with Caleb yelling, "I win!"

"Shhh." Ellie can be heard admonishing her cousin.

"I want to play the monkey game now!" exclaims Kathryn.

"Jah, we will play the monkey game Kathryn!" she is pulling it over and opens the lid upside down pouring monkeys everywhere. Kathryn falls back on the floor laughing while holding her stomach.

"Monkeys are everywhere! Look, look, monkeys are everywhere!" Kathryn squeals out still in a belly laugh. Everyone looks down at her and smiles broadly.

A hint of spring teases the day at sixty degrees this late afternoon. The men had just finished moving the baby furniture when the cloudy day turned into a light rain.

Looking past the Black Chevy Suburban parked parallel in front of the house they can see people moving about quickly on the city street, as if to run between drops.

Supper nears its completion. Freshly baked bread is out on the counter cooling, while the freshness can be smelled throughout the house. Having put the baby down for a nap Ellie and Susan are preparing a salad.

Elli is cutting tomatoes while cucumber lay on the counter. The two woman stand and talk next to each other, with a salad bowl in front of them. Susan is scraping carrots into the bowl.

"Tell me about your life in Ohio, Ellie."

"I feel relaxed here, alive, no stress," whispers Ellie as she looks over at Susan. "My husband is not who he let on to be when we were courting. He was so sweet then. Now he is mean. We cannot have children and he blames me. He yells at me for being baron. I do not feel that I am baron. I...."

Ellie throws her head back in anguish then down in tears, while without even thinking Susan takes her quickly into her arms and embraces her pulling her into her shoulders.

"My God Ellie, just...what is wrong? What has this man done to you for you to be in so much pain? Just leave him. No woman should be treated so. Many good men in the world and you're a good woman."

"I can't, my faith will not allow it. But...I like it here. I am so relaxed here. I sleep again at night. I smile again."

She picks her head up and stands arms length from Susan who still has her hands on Ellie's shoulders. She pushes a smile past her tears. She reaches up to her own shoulders places her hands on Susan's and smiles.

"Danki, Susan, you are a gut friend."

Susan with welled eyes herself smiles back and shakes her head yes leaning forward giving her one more hug.

Both women now turning back to the salad as Susan quips, "Tom seems to have an eye for you." They both laugh and look at each other. Susan continues, "Just saying," they just look at each other again and smile then giggle, as Ellie with now a mischievous smile quips, "You are so bad Susan Bennet," says Ellie, biting her lower lip.

Ding, the timer on the oven sounds.

"Dinner is done, jah!" The front door can be heard opening and closing.

"Daed!" sound the children, and the baby begins to cry.

"Let me attend to the baby, please Ellie," implores Susan with a smile.

"Jah, go ahead. Samuel we are back here!"

"Good evening sir," welcomes Lieutenant Bennet as she passes Colonel Samuel Hersberger, home from the hospital.

cccccccc

"Frau Hersberger, guten Abend, wie geht es dir. Ich bin Colonel Dreisigacker. Ich weiß, dein Ehemann. Wir sind Freunde aus Fort Bragg," says Colonel Dreisigacker while introducing himself.

Staring at first, Mary responds initially in German then changes to English, "Wie gehts, I'm Mary, you say you know Samuel from Fort Bragg and you're friends. Are you from Germany Colonel?"

"Yes Mary, I am liaison with the German Army, we work together, our forces." Laughing, he continues, "I was his reason for speaking German I think."

"He told me about this, when we first met, while out to dinner," thoughtful she continued with her fond memories, "our first date."

"I thought I would stop by, I was told Samuel might be here but he is not."

"He just left; he's probably at our home here in the city."

"I will catch him there then. I am so glad to meet you. I saw your baby earlier, strong boy, Jah?"

"Jah, danke Colonel. Colonel, do you have another name you go by?"

"Jah, Kurt."

"Kurt, es ist schön, Sie kennenzulernen."

"Mary, it is nice meeting you also."

Chapter Twelve

3 February 2002, it's cold out on the ramp to the emergency room this Tuesday at 11 am it is an overcast morning and a cold 37 degrees.

"They are ten minutes away. We should go down now," says the Army medic jingling keys in his hand as he walks over and opens the door to the Ambulance. He rubs his hands together, and then blows into them. A mist rises up from the enclosure.

Samuel is already seated in the front as Colonel Corrigan climbs into the back.

"Specialist, we can leave now," she says, looking over her right shoulder and giving a grin.

ccccccc

Waiting next to the tarmac at Andrews Air Force base they await the Biz jet. It now can be seen in the distance closing on the runway. *I've missed you liebe*, Samuel thinks to himself.

The aircraft is a few feet from the ground. Some birds nearby fly off, scattering as dust in the wind. The aircraft touches with a screech of its tires as it makes contact. It passes patches of snow left over from piles that had been blown there from plows as they cleared the snow from snow falls past.

They watch as the small jet taxis back and come to rest at the hanger where they wait with the ambulance.

cccccccc

"You're home," yells Samuel. Smiling broadly she stands in the doorway of the aircraft. A slight breeze picks her hair up whipping it around.

"Samuel, watch me," she says with excitement in her voice. She takes hold of the rails. And with the steward behind her slowly makes her way down the stairs. She is met by the medic who without touching her places a hand under her arm, as she reaches the last step and unto the tarmac.

"I flew today; Shhh....don't tell anyone....I like it a lot..." She looks into Samuels eyes, wraps her arms around his neck and kisses him deeply.

"I love you so much Samuel Hersberger. How are all of our four kinner?"

"Gut, liebe....verra gut....Jah." Still face to face he returns her kiss fully.

"Hi Mary, you look very well, exclaims Dr. Corrigan with a grin.

"How do you feel?"

"Gut! Last night I went to sleep. My feet were warm for the first time in my life! I am walking on my own. I'm a little unsure at times but I feel verra gut! Jah, I feel verra gut!"

"Well, let's get you back and checked out, I think you are going back to your house. We can see you outpatient now, how's that?"

Mary and Samuel still in an embrace, look over at the doctor pausing.

"This is good news, Colonel."

"Jah, verra gut news," says Mary in a low tone.

"I am thankful to our Lord for my healing, and to you, doctor," continued Mary.

cccccccc

"Mamm, are you staying with us? When are we going home? Can we go riding when we go home? I missed you mamm," asked many little voices, as Mary stood on her own inside of the brick home in Washington.

The loudest voice of all did not say a word. She stood motionless and quiet staring straight up. And out of nowhere....

"I love you mamm."

"Kathryn, I love you too, verra much."

A slight smile showed on Kathryn's face. Then she turned around and ran off.

"Wait, Kathryn!" Rachel called and ran after her sister. Caleb, silent, was close behind.

cccccccc

"Here is your coffee, Colonel," Lieutenant Bennett dressed in a pair of tan slacks and white blouse bends over and lays a tray of cookies with coffee down in front of Samuel and Mary.

Sitting on the back sun porch of their colonial home, away from home, Samuel has arranged for some alone time with his wife.

The solarium is full of large green plants and flowers which contrast the scatterings of white outside lying melting within the confines of high brick walls.

Trees without leaves canopy the very small back yard that the two longed loves look out at now.

"How about I tell you a story," begins Samuel with a smile.

"Jah, ok Samuel," says Mary quietly. She is sitting with her hair down and in a long pony tail. She has a simple skirt on with a blouse.

The children are away with Ellie for a walk this Friday the 29th of March. At 10am the temperature outside hinted of spring at 50 degrees.

Mary looks out through the glass walls at the trees with hints of spring in its buds. A masked cardinal looks down at them. A slight breeze can be seen moving the trees as the bird flutters its wings in response.

"I had completed just shy two years of college and had done gut. John's family told me I should go to a regular college. They told me I would do very well. I started shopping the internet and was looking for something different and challenging." Samuel looks over at Mary listening intently, as he continued.

"I found a college in South Carolina; it was near the beaches, mostly warm in the winter. The college of Charleston was nearby, lot's of girls there for a young person that I was back then.

They took me down and I visited The Citadel in February of that year. I stayed overnight. It was verra strict. But I was drawn to the challenge.

While I was there my knob that I stayed with told me that the U.S. Army was paying his way through college. I was intrigued." Samuel again paused to look and assess Mary by the look on her face.

Facing forward he began again. "In brief I did all the paper work, they like who I was in my character, background and I was accepted for that September by both The Citadel and the United States Army. They accepted one year of my education I started in my second year there, as a knob."

"What is a knob, Samuel?" asks Mary with a smile.

Laughing, Samuel responds, "That is what we were called, it is what we looked like with no hair," he stands and goes over to rub a brass door knob with his hand. He continued laughing with Mary joining him as she chuckled. Then he continued his story.

"I finished three years later and went into the Army. I went to officers basic for infantry; they are the ones to do the fighting mostly. I did very well and I then went to Ranger school.

I led men in a ranger battalion and then I went to Special Forces. I was there, Fort Bragg, until I left to come home. I spent 10 years there.

I was assigned to special operations and the newly formed Delta force while I was there. When I left I was in charge of First Special Forces Operational Detachment Delta. One of the primary missions of the unit is antiterrorism. Mary, do you have any questions?"

Mary stares, smiles at him and simply say's, "my David, no more Goliaths for you.

How were you injured?" Mary's smile disappears as she looks down at her right hand holding Samuel's.

"We were on a mission to look for a particular terrorist. An explosion occurred I was hit with a piece of shrapnel....ah, a piece of metal cut into my shoulder. I woke up in an Army hospital." Samuel pauses briefly and just as he planned.

"How would you like to go south and visit my school and Fort Bragg? From there we can visit Florida also. There is an Amish community in Sarasota, Florida."

"I will go anywhere with you, as long as I am with you Samuel. The kinner will see the ocean for the first time also, jah? I also have a friend there. My friend Sherry is there, we can visit. I can write her, but how can I receive a letter from her."

"Have her send it here and I will have it intercepted for us," replies Samuel."

"Gut, Samuel, Danki," smiles Mary.

Samuel say's with a broad smile while clasping tighter to his wife's hand.

"Jah."

"Samuel, our God of the Old Testament is alive today and David of the Old Testament, he is also alive today, in many ways and in many people. I understand this now, Samuel."
"I think now I will quickly write this letter to Sherry," as she goes and finds paper and pen and returns to the solarium.

Willard N. Carpenter

Dear Sherry,

Hope all is well with you. Sorry I have not been in touch. I was under the weather for awhile. Well, I guess that is a nice way of saying it. I actually had a stroke. I am still having trouble accepting it. But, I am feeling much better now. No problems as a result. I feel blessed. I am sorry that you were not able to attend the wedding. It was beautiful, as you can imagine, but I understand how difficult it is for you to travel with the children. Samuel thought it a good idea to get away for awhile and relax. So we are on a road trip down south along with the children, Susan, Samuel's personal aid and Ellie.

The children have never been to the beach or seen the ocean. They are really excited. I have given up counting the times that they have asked me, "Are we there yet" I don't want to impose, but I was wondering if it would be possible for us to visit?

Samuel has reserved hotels rooms for us down there, so I was thinking it would be fun if we could spend the afternoon together at the beach. The kids could play and we could catch up. I would love to see them, find out what's new with you and show you some wedding pictures. Please write back as soon possible.

Thanks,
Mary

Chapter Thirteen

"Ellie, the colonel and Mary are still out in the solarium, I'm going to leave shortly," informs Susan, as she crosses in front of the front door, the door bell chimes a classical tune.

"I'm here, I'll get it," she calls out reaching out and grabbing the door knob, she opens the door, "good evening ma'am, are you looking for Colonel Hersberger?"

"No, actually I'm calling on Mrs. Hersberger, would you let her and the Colonel know that Colonel Ryan, Elizabeth Ryan is here to visit," the Chief Nurse from the hospital is now standing in the foyer.

As she waited, Lt Bennet comes back, "the Colonel asks that I bring you to the parlor. Would you like a cup of coffee ma'am?"

"Yes that would be nice, thank you. You are?"

"I'm sorry, I'm Lieutenant Bennet. I am the Colonel's aide. I'm from Fort Bragg, Ma'am."

Willard N. Carpenter

"It's nice to meet you lieutenant, where do you hail from?"

"I'm from Pittsburgh, PA."

"Ahh, that's good country, steel country. Good baseball, Good football. Nice vistas. I visited their once," colonel Ryan continued chatting with the young Lieutenant. She sits as Ellie, brings coffee into their guest.

"Hello, I'm Ellie, I'm Samuel's niece," greets Ellie.

"Ellie, hello I'm Elizabeth, I work at the hospital that, your aunt? Am I correct? Yes your aunt was at. I'm...." As she is sitting amongst the young woman Mary walks in under her own power slowly but straight.

"Mary, hello it is so good to finally meet you. I must apologize for this intrusion. I have tried visiting many times before, but you were always involved. Today on my way out I made up my mind to visit you where I thought I could finally reach you. Colonel Hersberger, I'm Colonel Ryan, I would like for everyone to call me Elizabeth though. I'm the chief nurse at Walter Reed. Can we all sit?"

"Yes, let us all sit. Ellie where are the kinner? Can we bring them here?"

"Yes Uncle Samuel," Ellie responds as she leaves to get the children.

She returns only a moment later telling them to sit, "kinner sit here on the floor." Caleb in true boy fashion plops down in front of his mamm; Rachel though runs to and jumps into the lap of her father, while Kathryn slowly climbs onto her mamm's lap where she snuggles into her bosom.

"The boppli is asleep, Aunt Mary."

"Ahh, I've seen your son several times at the nursery," beams Elizabeth, while lifting the coffee to her mouth and taking a sip carefully as steam can be seen raising from the cup.

"I'm so sorry, would you like some cream or sugar for your coffee?"

"Ellie, this is perfect, hot, black and most importantly fresh! This is very Refreshing, from my standpoint." Ellie smiles at Elizabeth's comments.

"Young man, what's your name?"

Caleb stares at the English woman in the strange green uniform. She sits up very straight in her skirt with crossed legs off the side, in a very proper fashion.

"I'm Caleb, Caleb Hersberger. I'm Amish."

"I know dear, it would interest you to know that my great; great grandmother was also Amish. Ahh you are surprised," she puts her free hand up in front of her mouth.

"Yes, she was old order Amish from Lancaster. Sweet Heart, what is your name, you look so tired,"

Elizabeth is smiling over at Mary, looking at the young one as she looks away from her mother.

Perking up quickly, "I'm Kathryn!"

"Well, you are Kathryn, and very much awake!" Everyone in the room laughs.

"And daddy's girl, there. Your name is what sweet pea."

Kathryn blurts out, "I'm daed's girl too!"

Putting her hand up in front of her face as though embarrassed, "yes you are, and you thought I forgot, I didn't! I'm just speaking with your sister." Smiling she turns back to Rachel.

Rachel continues, "Kathryn is like that sometimes, Caleb does that more." Everyone laughs at the children. Samuel squeezes Rachel tight as Caleb smiles up at his dad.

"Mary, I have heard so many things about you and your family. I wanted to come and wish you well and our continued prayers for your continued recovery. We, as much as we certainly would not like to see you in any hospital am glad that we were able to be a positive means to you and your families health. Mostly Mary, it has been a pleasure getting to know your family and hearing about them. Personally it has brought back a piece of my history. To someone my age, that is very important." She smiles at Mary and over at Samuel.

"Colonel Hersberger, I understand you are preparing to leave shortly, If there is anything I or we can do to help you with any last minute preparations. If there is anything I can do to help you before you leave, please let me know."

"Elizabeth, thank you for visiting, this has been enjoyable. I will certainly do that and you have our and my thanks.

"Do you plan on going home?"

"No, actually we are going to do a bit of traveling."

"We have friends between here and Florida. Let's see, Fort Bragg, Charleston, South Carolina, Then the Sarasota, Florida area."

"What's in Charleston?" Elizabeth asks. Eyes shift back and forth as all are intently gathering for the most part, new information.

"Where I went to school? The Citadel."

"The Citadel, Ohh, A school with quite a good reputation. Very hard I would imagine though."

"Hardest," responds Samuel with a blank and longing stare.

"Ma'am my mother is a nurse, in Pittsburg, she works pediatrics. She is a nurse manager there."

"It is quite the admirable profession isn't it Lieutenant? You must be so proud of her."

"Yes ma'am, I am," says Susan with a momentary blank stare, as she pictures her mother.

"Where did you attend school?" Elizabeth continues to question.

"I'm also a Citadel grad," responds Susan enthusiastically.

"You are?" Elizabeth exclaims as she questions. Samuel surprised, turns towards her.

"I didn't know that Susan, you were one of the first women then! You had more to overcome. I thought I had it hard, I'm certain you had it much harder.

"Yes sir, class of 2000, it was hard, and being accepted was the hardest part. Though my peers, they were too busy to give me a hard time."

"Well Lieutenant, I'm impressed, but just like anything else, it will take a little getting used to but it will level out. I should imagine they will have numbers somewhere in the hundreds one day.

"Yes sir. Thank you, sir!" Susan shyly puts her head down, smiling. Then looks up "Don't mention it. You moved up very quickly!"

"Yes sir!"

"Well, I do not want to overstay my welcome," says, Colonel Elizabeth Ryan as she stands while brushing down her skirt. "Colonel Hersberger, Mrs. Hersberger, it has been very nice meeting all of you finally." After shaking Samuels hand she steps forward and hugs Mary, very strongly as she whispers, "it is so good to meet kin, Mary." She straightens and smile at her then looks down at the rest of the children and smiles broadly. "Lieutenant, tell your mother of our conversation will you. I love ties." She shakes Susan's hand.

"Yes maam, I'll be sure to do that," responds Susan.

"Elizabeth it is nice to meet you, but I have to get these kinner to bed." Mary is picking up a now sleeping Kathryn, who she drapes upon her shoulder.

"Of course, Ellie it is also nice to meet you."

"Jah, Danki, I will get the other two Aunt Mary."

The door opening, Colonel Elizabeth Ryan leaves. She looks out onto the night sky of the quiet suburban street. The only noise is the wind moving through the empty gray tree to the front of the house. She walks a short distance to her car up the street to the right.

A soft cool breeze blows through picking up First Lieutenant Susan Bennett's short brown hair. It tosses as a couple of guys in blue jeans and t-shirts look on from a distance.

"Colonel, I am going to leave now, I'll see you in the morning."

Coming from around the corner, "Susan, good I'll see you in the morning. How is your stay, your assignment with me? Can I get you anything?"

Susan smiling, looks behind her and smiles as she is pulling on her wool coat. "No sir, it's been a pleasure getting to know your family and helping in any way that I can."

Giving one more shake of her head she steps out into the now cool breeze which bites at her. She flips her hair back and from her face, as her pace quickens.

She is still being watched from afar as the 2 guys track her. She notices as she arrives at the black Chevy Suburban. Crossing to the front of her vehicle she stops momentarily and stares, while reaching into her purse, pausing, and then removing her keys.

Chapter Fourteen

A chilly 44 degrees this Sunday morning at 11 am on April 7, 2002. The sun peaks it's brightness through the trees giving hints of the spring that is upon them, a spring which promises warmth; a spring which promises brightness, in the hopes of a family which can now leave behind many chapters of a foreboding darkness.

Bundled against the chilliness, the family attended worship service at a non denominational church. There are no Amish communities nearby to find a church that they can go give thanks to a gracious and loving God.

Samuel's family is dressed plain again. Mary is in her black shawl and bonnet. A wisp of blond hair shows on the left side. Samuel has decided to also dress plain. Missing is his beard as they climb into the black suburban.

Ellie and Mary climb into the very back with the baby in a car seat in between them. In front of them sit Katherine between Caleb and

Rachel. Lieutenant Bennett and Samuel are in the front with Susan driving. Susan wears tan slacks with a white blouse. Her purse is kept near in the front seat.

Having eaten after services they start out for Fort Bragg. The bassinet is the last item to be packed; it lies on top of luggage neatly and carefully packed high and wide in the back of the Suburban.

cccccccc

The trip along Interstate 95 moves very quickly. Susan has been noticing an old blue pickup truck following at a distance through Virginia and around the belt way of Richmond.

As the Black government vehicle closes in on North Carolina, the pickup truck is now close enough where Susan looking in her rear view mirror can now make out the two guys.

It is the same two scruffy looking guys that she saw when she left the Hersberger home at night the week before.

"Sir, I have to bring something to your attention."

"Susan, what's up?" He looks over at her. "Two guys in a blue pickup?"

"Yes sir," Susan responds while looking up in the rear view mirror again.

"They have been at it since Washington. Well let's see what their intentions are. Slowly pick up speed to 80, let's see if they tract us."

At 80 mph the blue pickup is left behind, then in a short period of time it closes in on them to within 200 feet and stays.

"Hmm, you see that Lieutenant?"

"Yes sir, next step slow down to 45, just above the minimum speed limit. We'll let them pass."

As they slow down drastically Mary becomes concerned. "Samuel, is everything ok?"

"So far, we'll see, just be calm. Susan up here has everything under control." Samuel doesn't turn around but rises out of his seat and leans back a little while speaking to his wife.

Whispering now, he talks to Susan, "it's working here they come...they are forced to pass. Don't look Susan, stay the course."

"Yes sir, I know the drill."

The pickup truck speeds by and leaves them behind. As they drive for the next half an hour, there is no sign of the blue pickup truck.

A sign shows, Fort Bragg 86 miles. They pass under an underpass then pass an on ramp. They are driving where woods are.

Speeding up from behind, the pickup truck speeds up to three feet from the bumper. "Sir!"

"I see them! Everyone in the car remain calm. Susan, drive your drive. I'll call 911."

"Sir, my purse! Open it!" Opening her purse he stairs.

"Always prepared, lieutenant?" He pulls the U.S. Army service issue 9mm with holster from her purse.

Pulling the weapon he removes the magazine, and clears the weapon. Snapping the magazine back in place, he questions, "How many mags lieutenant?"

"One in the weapon and two spares in the purse." Susan doesn't take her eyes off the road in front of her, occasionally glancing up at the rearview mirror.

"Keep your speed at the limit," Samuel instructs.

"Yes sir!"

"Samuel, the men in the truck are back and so close. What do they want?" Mary now in a panic calls forward from the third row of seats.

As she calls forward, Kathryn can be heard whimpering, as well as Rachel. Caleb with wide eyes stretches up looking up and around.

"I don't know. Everyone just be calm."

"911 what is your emergency?"

"My name is Colonel Samuel Hersberger; I am with my family in a black GMC Suburban with U.S. Government plates. We are being pursued....stalked by unknown men in a blue, approximate 1989 Ford pickup truck. We have tried evading within the past two hours and they are back and within 1 yard of our rear bumper."

"Sir, any reason they may be following you?"

"I am a colonel with Special Forces, I hope that this is not the reason, but we shouldn't chance it at this time."

"Stand by Colonel, stay on the phone."

"What mile marker are you at colonel?"

"Hold one, 101. I'm notifying my superiors. I'm putting you on the phone with my aide, Lieutenant Bennett. She is driving; she is also military police and is armed. Notify state police of this."

"Yes sir."

ccccccc

"This is Lieutenant Bennett."

"Ma'am we would like for you to remain on the phone. Where is your weapon?" asks the 911 dispatcher.

"Holstered, lying on the seat under my right leg." Lieutenant Bennett responds as she uses her right hand with phone and checks the location.

"Keep it there." The dispatcher cautions.

"It's not going anyplace."

Tires squealing, the pick up now pulls up next to the car, the man in the right seat with scruffy face and dirty white t-shirt is looking and laughing at Susan.

cccccccc

When Samuel leans over and into view he is gestured at by the man who is using his right hand at the plain dressed man.

"Chris we are on the phone with North Carolina State Police. We are being pursued by two unknowns in a blue pickup."

"Sam, where is your location?"

"I-95 south....Mile marker....93 and closing at 65 miles per hour." Squealing of the tires and the truck again is right behind them near the bumper again. Rachel screams, and Kathryn is crying loudly.

"Were those squealing tires causing the kids to scream?" A tense General Hutchinson can now be heard.

"That's affirm."

"Sit under control as it stands?"

"That's affirm."

"How's the young Lieutenant."

"Gut," says Samuel, slipping back into his tongue.

"Don't hang up.... stay on.... these guys are about to have a regretful day. We have a team training, watch for a little bird and a team and notify state police on your end. We are going to handle this as a potential terrorist."

"Affirmative, will notify state police."

"Slow to 40, there is a deep curve at mile mark 85. Have state police intercept at the onramp at mile mark 85.2."

"Affirmative mile mark 85.2, police intercept."

cccccccc

"Let me have the phone Susan, we have a plan."

"This is Colonel Hersberger; we are going to handle this as a potential terrorist situation. State Police are asked to hang back and intercept us at mile mark 85.2. A special operations team will intercept at mile mark 84.8 request roads be cordoned off in all directions from that point."

"Hold one Colonel....State Police will comply with your request. They will have two cruisers wait on the ramp at exit 55. You are already being shadowed at a distance. Those chase cars will continue to clear all traffic behind you."

Chapter Fifteen

Six hours and a few minutes from Lancaster, Jacob Grau has a large farm near the intersection of Smokey Lane Road and Hickory Drive. Ellie his wife has been away for more than a month now writing to her husband once a week about what is going on.

The balance of their time away she informs him will be no more than two weeks from the seventh of April.

Jacob, an angry farmer, husband and neighbor can be seen in town having coffee and being pleasant to only one, a woman who he had met while walking along the road from the southern part of town to the northeast.

It was during a time when the leaves of the small amount of trees in this village of farms began to fall in crimson colors.

Sugar Creek, on this day is 54 degrees. The usual fields of corn rows lay baron and hard after the previous winter.

A slight breeze gives off little gusts of warmth with little hints of hope for the coming season of crops.

After the coldness of winter, the people of an old unchanged history begin to mimic the clouds above. Sometimes there would be none, and then as the day wore on, more would be seen moving slowly from one point to another.

They are untouched by their surroundings. Some children can be seen early in the season of hope without shoes already.

On this day open horse and buggy can be seen with young couples again moving with the clouds, lightly, from one unknown point to another.

On this day some play volleyball, others horseshoes, yet others will be found at a local singing, hunting for, hoping for, and seeking out those eyes of blue.

Freckles that are continually dreamed of will finally be kissed and nuzzled. Smiles which he can't take his eyes off of will finally be met with his own as they come together in warmth.

She will finally feel the strength of those arms she has wondered about since she started noticing such.

On this day Jacob Grau doesn't have his wife in mind, he wanders with his mind and lusts with his eyes, knowing that an all-knowing God sees him from afar yet he cares not.

He rationalizes away his future, blaming all on what was promised. He rationalizes that she is enjoying herself amongst the English. He rationalizes that she is baron, no good for anything. His anger builds each and every new day to today.

He forcefully takes this young unasked needy woman into his arms.

Without thinking of his yesterday and tomorrow, he kisses her. She hesitates and pulls away, running, being seen by many eyes as there are stones underfoot.

She doesn't notice the pain of her feet as they contact broken stalks, small stones and some telling thorns. She doesn't notice the blood from between her toes as her feet carry her faster and further from something she wants to forget.

Holding her dress up slightly, she cries, as she realizes what God has seen and prays for forgiveness. She runs and now pauses, screaming in the middle of a fallen corn field. Only the vast emptiness hears her aguish.

Running into a small wooded area her head falls in guilt and she sees again fallen crimson leaves.

Fallen crimson leaves crunch at each step while tears stream down rippling against her feet and making decorative splashes of red and yellow mixing with clay in her toes.

cccccccc

The angry not so young man is seen by the many same hidden eyes as stones, kicking, talking to himself screaming as he leaves an angry trail to his land and house. He slams the door, behind him as glass breaks and he realizes he will have to find an explanation for this.

What lie now among many he asks himself and again he rationalizes; Ellie amongst the English only her dreams matter. Who is this woman who defies me and Gods plan for me? Who is this woman? Who is this woman who denies me kinner and my dreams?

He throws the nearest thing, a coffee cup, at the door striking the top window. More glass is thrown out this time louder as the cup coming upon the wood of the porch landing with a thud.

"Heh Jacob! Wie Gehts," is heard a loud voice from the porch.

"Who is there," yells Jacob, stomping to the door opening it gruffly.

"Bishop Zimmerman. Jacob Grau, you can't hide from man how do you hide from God? You don't! I will say this one more thing. You have much to confess to God and your frau." He gently closes the door behind him and leaves.

Jacob, thinking to himself, I have nothing to confess, old man. My frau does. She will beg for my forgiveness. She will reap what she has sown here today, jah she will. She will bear me a boppli. There will be no rest for this woman until she comes under submission. This woman who ran from me, and she thinks she is so special? She is Baron of heart and why she has no one.

Again outside the little village of Sugar Creek, along the open bare roads of turned old corn rows, quiet returns. God's quiet. A soft wind blows toward the south east. The God of the Old Testament is alive this day in this small village of God's people of the New Testament.

Buggies go by and some give a short glance then ignore this house of Jacob Grau's. Life goes on. It waits with longing for the return of the sweetness of Ellie Grau.

Crimson leaves remain, now untouched but stained by a woman in her need, blinded. Crimson leaves remain, and they toss in the slight wind toward the south-east, toward Ellie Grau, calling to her.

The fall of Crimson leaves call you to unfinished business in your otherwise quiet community of Gods old people of the New Testament, Ellie Grau.

Chapter Sixteen

"Lieutenant, mile mark 86, ready?"

"Yes sir!"

As they pass the mile mark, the truck continues to pursue zigzagging back and forth in torment of the occupants.

"Colonel we have you patched through to the state police sergeant, go ahead"

"Colonel Hersberger, are ya ready to put this to an end?"

"Let's get this done," responds Samuel. He raises his voice slightly to his family in the car. "Police are coming, and the bad men will be stopped. Everyone be calm. It is about to get exciting and a little scary."

They pass the underpass of exit 55, three trooper pursuit cars come from behind at high speed boxing in the truck from behind lights are flashing as well as a myriad of sirens screaming.

The two North Carolina state trooper vehicles accelerate at high speed down the ramp to the front of the Chevy Suburban. As they enter the long turn the little bird helicopter can be seen coming in from on top of the trees just above the height of a car in front of the lead trooper cars which pass underneath them and stops.

"Colonel, have your driver slowly bring your vehicle to a stop and listen for further instructions."

"Got it! Lieutenant, bring the vehicle to a slow stop."

"Yes sir!" with the slowing a sudden thud is felt and heard against the back of the suburban. The children scream.

The little bird is now flying sideways with two heavily armed bearded men sitting on the floor of the side of the open door feet hanging down. They wear jeans with baseball hats and sunglasses; one gives a brief reassuring wave. He then waves for the suburban to pass underneath as it pops up slightly then ducks back down in front of the pickup truck.

The men can be seen with their hands out the window. State troopers from behind order the men out one at a time as the little bird is 20 feet in front of the now stopped truck. It is hovering six feet above the road surface.

Once the men are out on the ground the small helicopter with the four special operators turns toward the men who stick their head up to see the small but heavily armed gun ship land. Four armed men leave the aircraft with automatic weapons aimed at them.

"What the?" can be heard aloud from one of the men, the older man, driver.

The younger one who was gesturing from the passenger side is now crying. "What did we get ourselves into?" he says as he lies on the black top.

Four of the North Carolina State Troopers approach the two, they are frisked, hand cuffed and lifted and put against the truck.

"Sir, I really do have a thing or two to say to these two," says Susan Bennett

"Jah, I know," responds Samuel, they both exit the vehicle as the troopers from in front of them come back.

"You two ok, who is Colonel Hersberger?"

"I am," responds Samuel to a very confused and inquisitive sergeant. "Everyone in your vehicle ok Colonel?"

"Jah, a little shaken, but ok."

"These are the same two that I seen outside your residents in Washington, Colonel," says Lieutenant Bennett now half way to the two men.

"Yes it's them," she continues as she reaches them pulling out and showing her own badge. "May I have a moment?" she asks.

"Yes maam, the sergeant says."

Walking closer and nose to nose she looks up and into their eyes.

"Not so big now are you? Terrorizing woman, children and a peace loving family? Makes you a big man? No, not so big," she finishes when the bigger, older guy looking down on her spits on her right shoulder. He is taken down with one knee. It was swift, but decisive. She follows with grabbing his hair stooping over and looking right into his face and whispering, "This is my favorite blouse. This country is at war and you two are being looked at as terrorists. Think about it. Think about it long and hard."

"Did you see that? Ugh she kneed me," yells the older man.

"See what, asks the sergeant?" He just gives a grin, while looking at the young lieutenant. "What's your name, ma'am?" he asks Lieutenant Bennett.

"Susan Bennett, First Lieutenant Susan Bennett, military police, Fort Bragg."

"That was a nice piece of driving Lieutenant, nice piece! Kept your cool real well also, until now," laughs the trooper.

"He spit on my blouse."

"Remind me not to dirty up your clothes in any way now ya hear?" He continues to laugh. Susan now returns the laugh, shaking her head, as they walk back to the suburban together.

"Lieutenant, you good now?" asks Samuel.

"Yes sir, outstanding."

"Well I think it's time to get to Bragg don't ya think?"

"Yes sir," responds Susan as she enters the vehicle, she takes a moment to place her side arm in her purse, as she looks up at Samuel.

He chuckles and shakes his head, "always prepared, jah."

Susan turns around with Samuel; they look at the children who are very silent and wide eyed. "Wie-gehts?" he asks. All three nod their heads up and down.

"Liebe?" Samuel is looking at his wife, "you ok?"

"Jah, I am because of my 'David', Jah!" She now smiles.

"Ellie, you ok?" Asks Susan, also quiet but holding onto a reassuring smile as she shakes her head up and down in affirmation.

"Jah, I am ok, I have had enough with my time amongst some English today though."

Susan laughs, "yes me too! Let's get to the Fort."

cccccccc

The black Chevy Suburban arrives and takes a left unto Honeycutt road from Bragg Boulevard. What used to be an open fort is now locked down since the 11th of September the year before.

Security is heavy with a heavily armed Humvee sitting off the side. Security is made up of National Guard troops from Ohio who surround unmarked vehicles forced to pull off to the right. They drive to the gate on the left and identify themselves with appropriate ID cards which Susan and Samuel hand over. Not able to make out Samuel, they come to the passenger side of the suburban. Samuel already has his window down.

"I'm sorry sir I didn't recognize you right away. This is your family here?"

"Yes sergeant, my family is Amish. ID's were made without photos out of respect to the culture."

"Yes sir, no problem." The battle dressed military police sergeant waves the car through. It proceeds up Honeycutt to Knox Street. past Fayetteville state university offices on the right.

Off to the far right United States Army Forces Command headquarters could be seen as they make a left onto Randolph Street and away from headquarters.

Upon reaching the turning circle, Iron mike a WWII era big bronze soldier comes into view inside the circle. The children crane their necks in order to look at the large soldier. Susan stops the car off the side of the road, as Samuel looks on in curiosity.

"Susan everything ok?"

"Yes sir! With your permission," She unbuckles her seat belt and leans over the seat.

"Ok young uns out of the seat belts, I am going to drive real slow you can get up on your knees and look around. Sir?"

"Ok! Can you see now?" asks Samuel.

"Jah daed, smiling faces look around now."

Sitting back, Susan now continues Past Armistead St. then past Dyer continuing onto Randolph St, turning the large vehicle onto Alexander St. on the right. Susan slows the car as she sighs, taking in the familiar surroundings.

Chapter Seventeen

The beauty of the tree lined parade field comes into view on the left as they pull over in front of a large brick home on the right. It is very quiet.

"Ok, home for a week," says Samuel smiling past his nervousness.

He gets out of the vehicle and for the first time begins to lift and hug his children. They stare at the far expanses of the field.

"Wait here, kinner while we get your mother," Samuel quietly and methodically flips the seat forward, reaching in and first taking the baby.

He turns and hands Christopher to Susan, who longingly pulls Christopher to her bosom, close. Then he reaches in with his right hand and helps Ellie out.

As she steps foot on the ground for the first time she stretches, "Ach, feels gut jah. Long time in the car," she looks around, "it is beautiful."

Is this where people live here? Does everyone live like this?" Ellie continues to look around and take it all in.

"No, this is where officers live high ranking officers. This is a vacant house it is furnished, one of the few. Chris arranged for us to stay here."

"Sir, with your permission, when we are done here I am going back to my apartment, it's here on post," says Susan as she still cuddles the baby close to her.

"Yes Susan, but please join us for Dinner, ok? And by the way nice job today," says Samuel smiling at his aide.

"Yes sir, thank you!"

"Susan danke for all that you do for our family," says Mary now moving around as though nothing has happened to her. She is still holding onto Samuel's hand as they move away from the vehicle. Looking around she exclaims, "It is wunderbaar, jah!"

"Jah liebe!" A banging gets their attention as they hear a neighbors door two doors down close from behind them. Out from a short distant a slightly familiar face and woman with short brown hair comes towards them.

"Samuel, Mary wie geht's," calls out Colonel Dreisigacker, "Das ist meine frau, Bianca."

Mary, smiling remains quiet, as Samuel speaks up.

"Kurt, Bianka, wie geht's, das ist meine frau Maria."

"We are all fine Samuel, I met Mary in the Hospital, before I seen you."

"Jah, we met and it is nice to meet you Bianka," engages Mary as she continues, "you live here?"

"Jah, two houses down. We saw you arrive. Do you have dinner plans for later?"

"Only my aide, Lieutenant Bennet is coming over to eat with us. What did you have in mind Kurt?"

"We will feed everyone. We planned chicken schnitzel and potatos. Ist das gut?" asks Bianka.

cccccccc

Sunday evening, 6:30 pm, a large dining room table is set up. Then a smaller card table for the children is set with folding chairs. The smell of frying food can be made out beyond the front door of the living room, as the Hersberger family comes thru the front door.

Kurt is holding the door open. The TV is turned on in the living room on the left. In the distant to the right the dining room with the small kitchen behind that to the left. A small bedroom is right behind the kitchen.

Mary, Ellie and Susan make their way to the kitchen with basinet in hand.

"Bianka, wie gehts?" They find Bianka pounding a chicken breast with a frying pan, flattening it out like thin pieces of cardboard.

"What can I do," asks Susan as she places the Basinet with Christopher within sight of the entire women.

"Finish the salad?....I'm sorry...Hi, I'm Susan."

"Gut, Susan the salad, the lettuce is in the bowl, everything else is right next to it."

"I'm on it," says Susan picking up a knife and the peeled cucumber. As she picks it up she smells it, continuing, "I love the smell of cucumber."

"I have not cooked in so long, please, what can I do to help," asks Mary.

"Mary, the oil is hot; we will make the schnitzel fresh. Dip the chicken and dip it in the egg and then flour and lay it in the fry pan it on low so it will cook slowly and through," continues Bianka.

Mary is picking up each piece roughly as she is in charge of the chicken and familiar with its handling. The sound can be heard of frying as the piece is laid into place.

Ellie reaches in with a fork and pulls the ready piece out, placing it on an awaiting plate, smiling at Mary she says, "This is gut, jah."

Finished with beating chicken, Bianka excuses herself, as she opens the oven door. Pulling out a pan, she lays it on top of the stove lifting up the corner of aluminum foil. Revealed are roasted potatoes with herbs. The smell wafts through the kitchen and out into the living room.

"Was riecht gut meine liebe?"

"The roasted potatoes smell gut, liebe," responds Bianka lovingly.

"Wann ist abendessen?"

"Dinner is in 10 minutes lieb."

All the women laugh between the kitchen and dining room. A surprised look appears on Susan's face.

"Oh, I forgot the dessert in the car."

"What did you get?" asks Mary.

"I couldn't believe it at this time of year but I found strawberry short cake at the commissary. I got two they were small," finishes Susan with a giggle.

The three women look on, shaking their heads, when Ellie blurts out, "two jah, two is....gut!"

Again all the women laugh.

Bianca says, "It is possible the men won't want any, jah, possible."

"They don't have to know it's two," includes Susan again. They look at Susan and laughed even more as they shake their heads.

"Ach, I forgot the coffee," Bianka is thinking out loud to herself.

"I'll do that," says Susan.

"Susan, you are in the army yes."

"Yes ma'am," responds Susan looking on at Bianka inquisitively.

"No army coffee, Susan," the two laugh, as Mary and Ellie look on in curiosity.

"Army coffee is bad?" asks Ellie.

"Jah, sehr stark." Every one laughs.

"Susan reiterates, "no strong coffee." She giggles some more.

cccccccc

For dessert, both cakes were brought out, as the children looked on with, ahhhs. As they were preparing their individual coffees, the door bell rang. Kurt Dreisigacker answers the door.

"General, Mrs. Hutchins and Captain Hastings, how are you? We were just having dessert and coffee won't you join us?" asks the Colonel.

"Kurt, no one home at Sam's I figured they were here."

"Yes, everyone is here, we invited them so they didn't have to cook tonight."

"Good, good, so where is everyone?" asks Chris Hutchins as he rounds the wall towards the dining room, coming up behind Caleb.

"Were you a brave boy today?" he asks as he looks down and over at Caleb's face, while rustling his hair.

"Jah! They got the bad men," says Caleb smiling up face to face with the general.

"I know lots of excitement huh?"

"Too much..." begins Ellie looking up when her eyes come in contact with Tom's as he too rounds the wall into the dining room and the two lock eyes, for a moment. Ellie looks away, flustered. Ach, I am married what am I doing? Smiling she looks up, "May I get you coffee?"

"Hello everyone, Ellie how are you?" greets Tom.

"Gut! Jah, I am gut," responds Elli, now looking at Tom again, and again smiling directly at him. Just for a moment everyone looks at the two of them and as quickly as they did, they began cutting pieces of cake and pouring coffee.

"Everyone mentally survive their ordeal today?"

"Yes sir," responds Susan.

"Lieutenant, nice job under pressure today. The two that you helped catch is wanted in Virginia. The older man for assault and the younger for well let's just call it assault on women. Both are very bad characters, not terrorists but never the less bad characters."

Stunned silence consumed the room as the children ignored the conversation and continued to eat their cake and drink milk. Mary had misty eyes as well as Ellie.

"Thank you sir," responds Lieutenant Bennet in a respectful manner.

"We are not used to such things Chris," says Mary.

"You have a pretty good idea of what Samuels's job had been. Close up look at our operators at work."

"These men were soldiers in the helicopter today?" Asked Ellie

"Yes, they were," continued Chris. "some of this country's best."

Ellie laying additional coffee at the table steals glances at Tom as he is taking a chair from Kurt he returns her glances.

"I will take the kinner home, Mary. Kumme kinner, we left the door open, jah?" asks Ellie. She now walks over to the children, all with smudges of whip cream and strawberry all over their faces and all smiling wide.

"Jah, it's open. You are taking all four, this is a lot to do" says Mary.

"I'll help, I'll be glad to help," volunteers Tom getting up with his coffee in hand and taking a sip. "Save some of that cake for me huh," he implores as he longingly looks at what's left of the strawberry cake with pieces of the fresh looking large pieces of strawberries lying next to the rest of the cake.

"Ok, I have the baby," continued Tom, carefully lifting the baby.

"Well, as I live and breathe, look at that," says Chris.

"I'll deny it sir," laughs Tom, now looking down at the baby in one arm and holding the bassinet in the other hand.

"Just be careful with my namesake, Tom."

"Yes sir," says Tom as he is going out the door being held by Caleb. Kathryn is now being held by Ellie as Rachel holds her skirt.

As they walk the couple of short houses over, they stop momentarily and look over to the left at the parade field and the quietness of the night skies.

Ellie looks over at Tom, "god is gut, Tom."

"Yes he is, Ellie," responds Tom with a smile. Their eyes meet, and just for a moment Ellie's heart is warmed.

Chapter Eighteen

The Hersberger family is sitting around the table for breakfast. It's Monday morning. Samuel is dressed in his battle dress uniform. The rest of his family are dressed in their traditional dress, which in the chill of the air is comfortable. Susan had showed up early and joined the family for breakfast and she also was dressed in her battle dress uniform.

The refrigerator and cupboards were stocked; Eggs, milk, bacon, hams, orange juice as well as other items were in its place in the refrigerator. Mixes for cakes and cookies were in the cupboard as well as some other staples such as cereals, bread and some spices.

Breakfast was made by Susan and Samuel as they put together biscuits and sausage gravy, southern style. They enjoyed a chuckle as Mary and Ellie set the table while peaking around the corner at the children as they lay upon the floor playing the board games.

"Ach, I am so full, Samuel," says Mary.

"Jah, it is very filling, "says Ellie.

"Samuel, what are you and Susan up to," asks Mary as she smiles at her husband. "Why are you dressed in army uniforms?" she continues asking.

"You should be finding out momentarily," says Samuel.

"We are going to show you a little of our life today," adds Susan. As she finished her sentence there is a knock on the door.

"And now we can get started," says Samuel.

"Kinner we are going to have fun today, jah. You are going to do and see things not too many people get a chance to do," says Samuel as he opens the door to two soldiers with beards and in uniform.

As the soldiers make eye contact with Samuel they come to attention, saluting him.

"Good morning sir, ma'am as they eye Mary coming up from behind him.

"Transportation is here sir," says the sergeant.

Ellie is now standing up behind them as the second soldier sees her, "good morning ma'am," he says as Ellie smiles at the soldier.

From the distance at the Hum Vee can be heard a voice from another helmeted soldier, "good morning Sir. Mary, Ellie, good morning."

"Tom what do you say, are we set?"

"Yes sir!"

"Kinner, kumme, scnell!" Samuel calls to the children.

As they reach the door they are in aw, especially Caleb as the only words to escape his mouth is, "Daed!"

"Your name is Caleb, I'm Sergeant Jackson," say's the tall and senior of the two sergeants.

"Kathryn, you are with me," says Lieutenant Bennet as she picks up the little girl. As they walk towards the vehicle another young woman walks towards the house.

"Mary this is Anne, she is a specialist at the hospital she is also a mom and she is going to watch Christopher."

"Samuel, no!" Mary quickly retorts.

"Mary, the baby just ate, you have to trust me on this, Christopher has to stay here." Mary, not smiling just shakes her head.

"Ma'am if the two of you will follow me. He shows Mary and Ellie to the back door of the large military vehicle. The two climb up with the assistance of the soldier.

Samuel climbs into the front of the Hum Vee.

"Ok sergeant, let's go," says Samuel.

cccccccc

"General, two Hum Vees approaching," says the infantry major.

The two vehicles pull up next to an Abrams tank. The tank commander is sitting atop the turret and looking down on the two vehicles. The children are met by crew members of the tank.

"You want to go for a ride," asks the young specialist. He picks up Caleb who is wide eyed as he is passed up to the driver.

The helmet which is put on him swallows him up as he laughs. He is passed down into the turret.

Kathryn and Rachel are also passed up and Kathryn who is last has a helmet placed on her, she is giggling.

She is in the turret with the tank commander when the other hatch opens and the gunner pops up and Rachel comes up and like Kathryn is held up in place.

The turbine of the Abram tank whines and starts. As the children laugh, the tank lurches forward. It then picks up speed down the trail as the turret turns to the side, then backwards as the children laughing waves at the crowd behind them.

Samuel smiling broadly waves back and looking over at Mary and Ellie finds the same with them laughing and shaking their heads no at the same time.

"Welcome to Normandy drop zone ladies," welcomes General Hutchins. "Today we have a display already planned. You will be able to see firsthand how some aspects of the United States Army functions."

Ten minutes later the massive tank is going slow with the tank commander sitting atop the turret with his feet inside the open hatch.

The two girls with bonnet strings hanging down from under the over sized helmets are sitting on the turret with the sergeant with his arms around them holding them tight.

Caleb now is in the other hatch with a big smile. He can be seen pointing and holding his mouth piece up to him and talking.

"You had fun, jah?" says Samuel, as he is looking and calling up to his children.

He reaches up and brings down one child at a time as they go talking excitedly to their mom about what they did.

"Listen, do you hear that, listen now," teases Samuel. Looking up Samuel points.

"Ach, look!"

Everyone looks up as a large C17 jet aircraft pass from far above. Little dots begin to appear as chutes open up and get closer.

The little necks strain as they begin to point.

"Ach, daed and mamm men falling from the sky look! Look!" Excitedly Kathryn is jumping up and down, as the first of the soldiers; paratroopers hit the ground and gather up their chutes.

They move forward quickly as maneuvers begin. Gun fire erupts as the soldiers begin their exercise. Mary and Ellie have their hands over their ears.

"Samuel, did you jump out of planes like these men?" Mary is stone faced in disbelief of what she is seeing.

"Jah, gut fun," says Samuel excitedly.

When these men had moved on then helicopters could be heard as they quickly flew in and began dropping off more soldiers.
They could be seen lying on the ground. As the Black Hawks lifted off smoke began to appear on the field and more gun fire.

Automatic fire could be heard as well as explosions could be seen and heard. Mary could be seen with tears welling in her eyes.

"These men they do this, they prepare everyday for war. Many David's.... jah.... many David's."

"I think I understand now," adds Ellie. "Very exciting," she continues to add.

"Many David's," says Mary again.

Monday afternoon they spent exploring Ft. Bragg by their Suburban. They had gone to see the new Womack Army hospital.

They visited and shopped at the Post Exchange, sort of like a Wal-Mart. Then they went over to the commissary for grocery shopping.

They found churches all over the post also which they were surprised, but admitted that they shouldn't have been.

They learned what a bowling alley was and stopped into the sport center to let the children play.

They seen elementary schools and something they never experienced, a middle school and a high school.

The entire week was restful as was intended. Mary became stronger as each day came and went.

As the week came to an end, everyone was ready for what was next in the new adventure. As the week came to an end they learned who Samuel was, who he is, who he would be.

Chapter Nineteen

Mary's warmth could be felt through her night clothes as Samuel awoke cuddled to her back with his arm wrapped around her. Mary's feet, warm now were no longer needed in between Samuel's legs.

He kissed Mary's neck through her hair, then as he had many times before moved her hair, exposing a little of the back of her neck then nuzzled and kissed it.

"Mmm," sounded Mary, as she rolled unto her back. She looked up into Samuel's eyes, as he leaned up on his right elbow on his pillow looking down and into Mary's eyes.

"I have truly missed this Samuel; I have missed your warmth, your touch and your lips on my skin," whispered Mary. As she leaned up she is met again by his lips on hers.

Mary lies back, as she is followed by Samuel; he touches her face caressing it with his left hand. Mary pulls Samuel in close with her right hand around the back of his neck.

"I love you liebe," says Mary, breathing heavily with Samuel's face above hers. Samuel opening his mouth slightly kisses her again. Mary breathes in deeply. "I have missed.... you so much, Samuel."

cccccccc

The luggage is lined up, near the front door when the door bell rings at the Colonels residents. At the door are Captain Tom Hastings and General Chris Hutchins. Both men are dressed in BDU's (battle dress uniforms).

"Lieutenant is the boss around," asks General Hutchins.

"Yes sir, we are just about set to leave, won't you both come in," directs Susan as she steps aside allowing the two officers to step through.

"Thank you lieutenant," says Chris as Tom follows smiling at her and nodding his head.

"Sir, good morning," she acknowledges the Captain as he passes her.

"Is there a colonel in the house?" calls out Chris, kiddingly.

"Jah, I am here," says Samuel coming around the bend from the bedroom. Mary is with him hand in hand as they enter the foyer.

"Good morning Mary," says Chris addressing Mary.

"Well there, you have come a long way, I dare say. I hope your stay here and at Walter Reed has been good for you," continued Chris looking and smiling at Mary.

"Chris I don't know how I can say Danke, words don't seem enough," says Mary now holding unto Samuels arm.

"Keep giving my namesake a kiss on the forehead for me; let him know where his name comes from as he grows."

"Done," interjects Samuel putting his hand out to shake.

"You're a good man, Samuel," compliments the General now as he looks Samuel in the eyes.

"Thank you, sir."

With that said, Ellie comes in from the back yard with the children as the baby can now be heard from the basinet on the sofa stirring, then crying.

"Ach, wie gehts," says Ellie as she goes straight towards the baby wrapped in a blanket and lifting him. Tom meets her, looking at her as she continued.

"Well Ellie Grau, I guess this is it, I don't know if I will ever see you again but I will say it has been nice becoming friends with you," whispers Tom, as he stands bent over and within inches of Ellie.

It is wrong what I am thinking, jah it is. But I have...no I can't have these feelings,

Willard N. Carpenter

thinks Ellie as she turns her head towards Tom inches from his face. The attraction would be visible if anyone had been paying attention.

"I don't care that this is wrong, I will miss you Tom," she says as she nears his lips with her own then turning her head, *Lord my God help me with my temptations.*

She looks back at him with tears in her eyes, walking off with the baby in one arm and wiping her eyes with the sleeve with her other. She looks back and with her lips mouths again, "I will miss you."

Tom fighting back the moisture of his own eyes, simply smiles. Turning he looks back at all the going on of the foyer.

"Sir, I'm set," he says looking at his commanding officer.

"Samuel, Mary, safe journey," he says, looking over at Tom quizzically.

cccccccc

The black suburban passes over the North and South Carolina border as the children stretched up looking out as the car left the interstate via the off ramp.

As it turned into the parking lot of the South of the Border, Susan turned saying, "sir, with your permission, you can take your seat belts off and look around!"

The children were instantly up on their knees oohing at the giant Mexican hat. The car proceeded around toward the far side and toward the children's rides.

"Surprise kinner!" exclaimed Samuel.
The car came to a stop; all three children were gotten out of the car.

As the ride got started the girls who had never made a loud noise, screamed! Their faces were excited with eyes wide open!

The ride went around again and they continued to scream. The ride went around again and this time little arms were flailing in the air with their screams.

The ride went around again and they were screaming, "mamm and daed! Ellie! Miss Susan!"

Soon, all too soon for the children the fun came to an end, and the Black Suburban was back on the road. In just a short couple of hours it turned off Interstate 95 and turned east onto Interstate 26.

An hour later on the 15th of April, Monday, the Suburban reached and turned off and onto the Citadel exit. It preceded down a residential road pass a baseball field on the right.

As it came upon an old Lutheran church on the corner on the left hand side it turned right and made its way pass a city park on the right hand side.

As it approached Lesesne gate it turned left and away from the military college and arrived at the group of hotels three blocks away.

Samuel got a cluster of three hotel rooms, two were adjoining. The children were given one of the adjoining rooms with 2 double beds.

The sisters were in one and their brother another. Samuel and Mary took the other adjoining room with the baby and basinet on the second bed near Mary.

The third room was shared by Ellie and Susan who had become very good friends. They were looking forward to this time together. Susan could be heard excitedly telling Ellie about her former school, as they entered their room.

Chapter Twenty

"Colonel...Samuel said we were not needed until tomorrow morning, let's see that would be Wednesday, my days are getting mixed up. Mary is going to rest and they are going to have their meals here and enjoy the children during the day," says Susan as she enters the room, she can be seen smiling as she closes the door. It is as though something is up.

"Jah, I am not needed also? What are we to do? You have something in mind."

"Yes I do, it is going to be 77 degrees today and we are going to the beach!"

"I have never been to the beach! But what am I going to do there? I am going to walk around in this," Ellie is holding out her skirt from the side.

Ellie now has a disappointed look on her face. "Maybe this is not a gut idea," she now says with disappointment in her voice.

"Nonsense, we are going out today, and you are going to have fun. There is a little boutique downstairs, I am taking you shopping. We can find you something for the beach!"

"I can't, it isn't our way Susan," says Ellie very seriously. She then changes her mood as though a light just came on. "Do you think I can? Really! I can pay you back. Samuel has given me money." Ellie is now very excited.

"You are not paying me back, let's go!" Susan grabs her purse.

"Jah," says Ellie very excitedly. Her kapp string flies away with her own breeze she creates as they rush down the hallway together to the elevators.

cccccccc

After some stares in the boutique the workers go about their business and so does Susan with Mary as they make their way to the one piece suits.

"I have to try these on, this is a lot of work putting this on," says Ellie as she again holds out her skirt and apron.

"Ellie Grau you are not leaving this store in what you are wearing now, when we get done with you, you will be completely incognito. Your own family won't recognize you."

"I trust you, Susan," smiles Ellie

"Ok then, how do you like this one?" Susan pulls out a baby blue one piece bathing suit.

"Jah I like this, can I look at others?" Ellie is excitedly flipping through the circular bathing suit rack. She pulls out a yellow one piece.

"I like this, I like yellow," says Ellie with a broad smile. "But I don't know my size," she continues.

"Well, time to find out, first though we should find you a cover up and a cover for your head. Let's see this long skirt and a loose blouse that matches. How about this yellow flowered print? And here, this loose white blouse.

"Ach, I like this verra much, but this blouse I can see through it...over a bathing suit though... You think it is ok?"

"Perfect!" Susan is smiling and shaking her head affirmatively. "Now into the changing room," says Susan as she takes Ellie by the arm toward the changing rooms.

cccccccc

"This is I think...small, and I feel as though I have no clothes on, is there a bigger size" a concerned look over takes Ellie.

"Let me look at you," says Susan, standing at the door of the changing room."

You look wonderful; you are a beautiful woman, Ellie Grau."

"My husband doesn't think so," frown's Ellie, again with tears pooled in her eyes. She is far away again in a distant place of farm land and fallen stalks of old corn missed by the harvest.

"I quite frankly don't want to hear about your husband again, you're here now and today is your day," scolds Susan looking right at Ellie.

"Jah, Jah! It is my day. The sun is shining brightly, it is my day."

"Now is it comfortable to wear?" Susan continues to question.

"Jah, verra!" Excitement returns to Ellie's voice.

"Good then...Try it on...wait," Susan turns and summons a sales person.

"Miss...miss we can use some help. My friend here would like to wear these out."

"Sure we can do that, Just let me have the tags," says the sales person as she has Ellie turn around. "This looks really nice on you," she continues.

"Try the wrap now, this skirt looks really nice also!" Susan is turning Ellie by the shoulders, "look in the mirror, this looks really good."

She stands behind her holding her shoulders. "Ok I'm stepping out, blouse next," the door shuts as Susan walks away and is looking around...*Yes, this is it! Perfect!* She thinks to herself.

"Ellie, are you done?" Susan is again outside the door.

"Hurry! Open up!" She helps the door open. "Oh my, only thing left is this!" Ellie is turned by the shoulders.

The kapp, already lying on a small bench has been abandoned and now the tightly bound hair is being unpinned and let out and will soon be abandoned with it.

"Ach, what are you doing Susan, my hair is down only in front of my husband."

"Not today it isn't," laughs Susan as she lets Ellie's hair down and removing a brush from her purse runs it through several times.

"Ellie Grau you are beautiful, now let's put this on." She reaches up and places a bandana on the top of her hair, wrapping it under the back. It is also yellow of the same shade as her bathing suit.

"One more thing, she pulls Ellie out of the dressing room, to the counter she is taking all of this...scissors...yes this will do it!" The tags come off quickly and are given to the sales person.

"What do you think you like?" Susan has Ellie facing the sunglasses.

"Are you sure?" Ellie questions with a smile.

"Yes, which one?"

"These," she pulls out a dark framed pair.

"Good choice, let's see! Yes, I like these! Now let's look at the new you," says Susan as she looks at Ellie starting at her hair down to her feet under her wrap around skirt.

As she reaches her feet she pauses and starts laughing. "Oh my Ellie, how did you do all that changing with sneakers on?"

Ellie looks down, holding up her skirt to reveal her sneakers on over socks. "I didn't even think about them, I got so excited about everything I didn't even think about it. She starts laughing with Susan.

"Ok back to the changing room, off with the socks and shoes."

Sandals were gotten. All was paid for and the two being done were now off as they entered the large lobby area. As they entered they could see Samuel and the family entering the restaurant at the far side.

"Wait here at the elevators," says Susan running off to catch up with the family.

A minute later she returns with a big smile, jingling keys in her hands. The elevator doors opening, she ushers Ellie in quickly.

"We have the black beast to ourselves for the day," she says holding up the car keys and again grinning.

They are having a late breakfast and I am starving. I know a good place for breakfast, first I am going to change into my bathing suit, are you ready?"

Chapter Twenty-One

The two were striking as they stepped out onto the beach; Susan was wearing a two piece dark blue bathing suit with a one piece wrap around skirt.

They had breakfast at the Variety store, which sets along one of the many small piers in and along the James River in Charleston.

As they came onto the beach in Isle of Palm, there were more than a few people on this very hot and humid day of mid April.

"I feel bad," says Ellie with a mischievous smile.

"Hmm...bad it is then," says Susan as she takes her wrap off and lays it on her towel. Let me spray you or your going to burn.

"Burn?" Asks Ellie, as she cautiously removes her blouse and skirt.

"Here." As Susan sprays, a couple of guys walk by gawking. Susan looks over and smiles at them, then continues to spray. "There, all done," she says as she finishes up. "Here now get my back."

"Jah, just push the button on top," she says as she begins pumping the liquid onto Susan's back.

The wind kicks up a little off the ocean picking up Susan's short hair and brushing it across her face. As she pulls it out of her mouth a bigger gust pulls Ellie's long hair from at her waist and flings it into the air like a banner.

Pulling her hair down, she jerks her head bringing the remnants into control. As the two guys continue they turn and look over their shoulder of the girls spreading their two large towels out onto the sand.

Ellie closely follows Susan's lead. The two lie on their stomach looking at each other.

"How do you feel now Ellie," asks Susan again brushing a little hair from her mouth and reaching in to her beach bag and pulling a couple of magazines out.

"Here would you like one?" Handing over one of the magazines, she looks back over her shoulder. Ellie again smiles with a hint of a tear welled in her eye. "I feel so free right now. I feel bad too, like I am on my Rumspringa," she says while rolling onto her side.

"I have never had a friend like you. You make me feel good about myself. If I were to have met you during my Rumspringa I think I would not have been baptized. I would not have joined this church."

"Our beliefs are not so different, I too am a believer. But I do not believe that being here with you as a friend and being out in the sun is sin." Susan now turns onto her side to face her friend.

The sun continues its climb as the temperature continued to climb. The ocean breeze offered the only relief. Off in the distance a freighter can be seen preparing to enter the Ashley River.

A plane flies over pulling a banner advertising a local restaurant. White clouds can be seen spotting the sky.

"The wind feels good over my skin," says Ellie as she closes her eyes while experiencing the newness of the entire day. "I feel...what is a gut word...relaxed...is this so bad...Jah...I feel gut."

The two lie quietly not a few feet apart from each other. Their eyes closed the suns warmth washes over their skin. Sensing something or someone, Susan rolls back onto her back and hunches up on her elbows.

"Can we help you two," she asks the same two guys who walked by earlier. They stand in the sun and cast a shadow on the two women.

Susan still holds a hand over her eyes shadowing part of the sun which remains in her eyes. She is quiet awaiting an answer when one of the guys appears to gather courage.

"Hi I'm Randy and this is Tim, we go to school at the college of Charleston he says. We were wondering if you would like to spend some time with us," the taller of the two rattled on."

"No thanks, Randy. We would rather have some time alone."

"Ahh come on, ya aren't doing anything, no more than we are."

"I and my friend would like to keep it that way Randy. Again no thanks."

"I think, you're lonely for some company," says Tim as he stoops down.

"Here let me make this a little clearer to you guys," begins Susan, reaching into her bag, as she searches she continues, my friend here is married."

"Bull, she doesn't have a ring on," says Randy now stooping down.

"And I am a police officer," says an annoyed Susan while pulling out opening and showing her ID.

"And I am an Army Officer, a very annoyed Army officer, an annoyed Military Police officer. Now do you get it?"

The two rise up to a standing position, "I'm sorry ma'am."

"Wait a minute," says Susan, while standing also. "Are you two military?"

"Ahh no, well yes, yes ma'am," stammered the shorter of the two guys."

"We're sorry for troubling you ma'am."

"You didn't answer my question," reminds Susan, more sternly.

"We are, we are ROTC at the college, and we seemed to have made a mistake."

"You do know what your mistake is then?"

"Yes ma'am!"

"Be respectful next time boys, just a little respect goes a long way. Do you understand?"

"Yes ma'am," says both guys together.

"Dismissed," adds Lieutenant Bennet as an added measure of intimidation.

"Yes, ma'am lets go," says Randy elbowing Tim.

As the two left Ellie just lay on her side looking at and witnessing her friend at work.

"Can I take you home?" Kids Ellie approvingly.

Chapter Twenty-Two

"Ach...Samuel, you went to school here. It is so big. White castles everywhere," exclaims Mary, as she peers out from the front seat today as Samuel drives.

Susan is sharing a seat in the back with Ellie. Samuel begins his narrative, having passed through Lesesne gate.

"Lesesne gate, it has been a long time since I have been here indeed. I entered as a naïve young person just barely away from my Amish family and home," begins Samuel.

"I left behind the love of my family and my adopted family. I left behind four seasons. I left behind the Pennsylvania woods. I entered Lesesne gate. I thought I knew what hard was being Amish until I arrived here," he continues as he looks around.

"My first week; 'Hell week' they named that right. It separated those of us that really wanted to be here from those that did not or wasn't sure. Not only did I learn about myself in what I could stand physically but also mentally and yes spiritually. It is times like those days that try men or in my case boys. I remember," says Samuel deep in thought.

"Every living and breathing thing I did was watched so closely that I thought I would be punished for drinking in too much air. I come to miss everything from home then, my family, even the hardness of farm life. Anything that may have seemed hard when I left, I then yearned for. But yet I stayed. I was challenged by my new life in front of me."

"This was...verra hard time, my first year here," finished Samuel as he leaves his thoughts behind. At that moment a young female cadet is seen walking off the sidewalk in the gutter, she was ridged in her stature. She stood in an exaggerated attention and walked very fast.

"Samuel is that a man, and look how he is walking," says Ellie with Mary looking over. Susan giggles.

"That was me several short years ago," adds Susan as the large Suburban pulls into a parking space in front of the church.

"This is the avenue of Remembrance. I want to show you something," continued Samuel as he now got out of the car with the entire family opening car doors.

"See this building in front of us...Summerall Chapel. This is where I went to church...when I could," smiles Samuel as he remembered more of his time. "The names of those on front of the church are the names of those who lost their lives in the defense of freedom, who attended The Citadel."

"Many more David's Samuel? How many men have there been, giving their life? And they do so without a second thought as to why," solemnly Mary takes grasp as to the depth of what appears before her. Her face strained. No tears. She reaches up and pulls on the strings of her kapp.

"These are hallowed grounds. That cadet is a woman. She has hair. She is also a knob, a new cadet. She is in her first year and there are certain things she and other knobs cannot do in their first year. She has not earned the right to walk on the sidewalk on the avenue of remembrance. She also cannot walk across that parade field."

Another cadet rushes by, and as he does he passes an upper classman and salutes sharply with fear in his eyes as they strain in a pasty fashion.

Susan can be seen shaking her head, "just like yesterday...I don't even feel as though I left."

"I know what you mean," says Samuel looking around at her. They cross the street to the chapel and thru the arches. On the wall outside the chapel are plaques of alumni who have made the ultimate sacrifice.

Both Mary and Ellie walk up to the wall next to the door. Without saying anything to each other they reach up rubbing the plaques with their open hands.

"I will never look at the English the same again, Samuel," say's Ellie with tears in her eyes.

"I will not either, liebe," adds Mary.

Opening the great wooden doors they walk into the great old church with its Gothic wooden ceiling.

"What are all these flags," asks Ellie.
"These flags represent every state of the Union," answers Susan. "Remember when the Nation formed we were all individual 'little countries' which we now call states. They have their own identity and government," smiles Susan.

They peer over the wooden pews to the front, then left to the pews in front and to the side and right to the pews again facing center from the right side.

The children with their hands held all are looking with mouths wide open staring at the ceilings.

Having visited and sat for a moment in the front for prayer, Samuel lead his family and extended family out the back. He pauses momentarily to leave a check in the collection box.

It is 1 pm, walking the sidewalk they head for Mark Clark hall next stop on the Avenue of Remembrance. Looking left over the parade field he notices activity.

I wonder what is going on...it's Friday...weekly parade...after nearly 25 years...huh...150 years...just a different parade

Unveiling

field. This will be fun for the family the kinner will never forget this. Four o'clock use to be parade. Gut this is gut.

Walking inside Mark Clark hall they enter the lobby.

"Samuel, what is this place?" Mary asks while looking around. "Ach a store!" she continues. Mary makes a straight line towards the gift stores door.

"Ellie, you're with me," says Susan taking Ellie by the arm.

"I know your size now, let's see...a sweatshirt, what would you like?"

"Ach, Susan, you keep forgetting I am Amish, and soon I will return home.

"Keep your clothes folded up and in your suit case," interrupts Susan.

Again, Ellie smiles as she looks at Susan. Then leaning into her, wraps Susan in her arms, hugging her deeply.

"I shall always remember you, whispers Ellie.

"Remember me, as though I am going to lose track of you. Don't think so. You're stuck with this friend," whispers Susan into Ellie's ear.

cccccccc

Fifteen-thirty hours...time to head over to the bleachers. I won't say anything.

165

"Lieutenant, may I have a word," Samuel calls over to Susan who is with Ellie and now carrying the baby.

"Yes sir. But I am already on board with your idea," says Susan, smiling.

"Always prepared huh?"

"I try to be, sir."

"I couldn't ask for a better aide, Lieutenant."

"Thank you, sir."

"Susan, you have also become a gut friend."

"Thank you, sir...I feel the same way...thank you again," smiles Susan.

"No, thank you," replies Samuel, as they near each other in the parade field.

"Wie-gehts, Samuel?" asks Mary.

"You'll see, liebe," replies Samuel, smiling back at his wife. The children are running around the parade field. The girls can be heard screaming, Caleb is yelling and chasing after his sisters. Christopher is sound asleep in Susan's arms.

Reaching Padgett Thomas Barracks, Samuel brings his family to the front entrance.

"Samuel, this place is so very big," says Mary, looking inside the white stone structure, unto the expanse of concrete floors painted red and white in a checker board.

Cadets can be seen scurrying about in gray over white uniforms (salt and pepper). Some are carrying instruments. A cadet can be seen placing a trumpet to his mouth, playing out a few tunes.

"I lived here for four years, my room was up their the first year, the next level down the second year and the 3rd and 4th years it was right there straight ahead one floor up."

"I read plans are made to tear down this building and rebuild it. This year matter of fact," continued Samuel.

"I think I read the same article, sir," joins in Susan.

They sat in the bleachers, following the children to the top. The children stood along the railing as the bleachers now as filled as they were going to be settled.

The sound of bagpipes playing Highland Cathedral could be heard as it came up from behind the family from Padget Thomas barracks. They marched in between the bleachers and unto the field, followed by the Regimental Band, a total of about 70 players in all.

All was quiet, and again the children stared with mouths open wide while standing on their seats. The band came to rest at the left end of the field. An announcer began introducing the two bands and its leadership also the history and importance of music on the field of battle.

Afterward the band started playing and unto the field from approximately six areas cadets in grand formation began to come out onto the field and form on the opposite side of the bleachers. Close to 2,000 cadets wearing gray over white uniforms topped off with tall black hats called shakos which have plums of ostrich feathers atop them.

The National Anthem played and as it ended, Susan reached over and covered the babies' ears just as the artillery went off, surprising everyone, but Samuel and Susan.

Following a pass in review and the cadets leaving the field everyone stood and watched the band as it played, while also leaving the field.

The crowd had dispersed, Samuel remains seated with Susan as the children begin to look around.

"I will not return here, Lieutenant, do you think you'll be back?" asks Samuel now standing.

"I don't know sir, I should hope so, but there are times I don't miss this at all," says Susan with the rest of the family now looking on.

"Well, our time here has come to an end, we leave tomorrow."

"Yes sir," responds Susan again. Looking around, then again at Samuel.

"Are we leaving tomorrow, Daed?" asks Kathryn.

Samuel leaves his far away stare, returning he looks up at Kathryn and their other children, smiling at them.

"Jah, we leave tomorrow!"

They look around one more time while climbing down from the bleachers. As they start the walk across the parade field he hoists Caleb onto his shoulders. Caleb, losing his balance, reaches down and grabs his daed's ears.

"Sohn, those aren't reigns," says Samuel, laughing and reaching for his arms. "You won't fall, I won't let you fall," he reassures again.

Mary is excited to see her friend in Florida.

Sherry had written back to her friend Mary and all were excited to visit them in the Amish community of Pinecraft Florida. For the children they were more excited to see the ocean for the first time.

Chapter Twenty-Three

Although it was already warm in Charleston, as they left Georgia and entered Florida it actually began to feel hot. Opting to leave the car windows open while driving, warm air wafts through and through, throughout the car.

Making their way on I 95 with windows open Susan was again driving and Samuel was in the front seat. Mary sat with Ellie in the back with the baby.

Mary and Ellie had their head back with eyes closed, while the children looked all around the best they could. Looking up they could see palm trees, tops framed in blue with wisps of white. Streaks of brightness can be seen making its way through the palm leaves. As the car turned those rays make their way into little eyes staining against the brightness.

cccccccc

"Daed, I have to go," says Kathryn with eyes lit up.

"We are almost there," answers Samuel turning and looking over his left shoulder.

And with that the car turns into the high rise hotel just outside of Sarasota.

"Everyone wait in the car, Susan I'll be right out, I'm just going to check in," continued Samuel as he is half way out of the car. Looking at the front doors of the huge hotel, he hears that familiar warm voice.

"Liebe, ich will mit dir kommen wollen, warten Sie bitte," says Mary softly.

"Jah, please liebe come with me, jah I'll wait," smiles Samuel.

cccccccc

The car being unpacked for the last time the children all are looking out the front window, mouths open as they look down then out from the 12th floor of the ocean front window.

"Ach, mamm look," says Rachel; the three have hold onto each other, afraid of falling.

"I'm scared," says Kathryn holding onto Caleb's arm.

"Nichts zu befürchten Kind," whispers Mary, stooped down near Kathryn, as she looks down at the small people walking along the beach.

"Nothing to be afraid of, Jah mamm," says Kathryn reassured, yet holding tightly onto Mary's arm.

"Look at the ocean, the blue, the boats, the little people in the ocean," continued Mary as she to is amazed at all that was going on.

Little faces are now pressed into the glass leaving spots of fog on the once Chrystal of glass.

"Ach, mamm, we are far up," says Caleb on his tip toes head pressed against the glass looking straight down.

"Liebe," says Samuel coming in the door. He is quickly behind her with his hands in her hair, gently pulling her head back bending over and kissing her fully. All three children look over and smile. Mary smiles while rising to her feet and turning to meet her Samuel wrapping her arms around his neck.

"I love you, Samuel," she says.

"I love you too, very much, more than I think you will ever know," he kisses her again fully while brushing the side of her face, wrapping his finger in her hair and pulling her into him. A pulling on his pocket brings Samuel and Mary's attention back to the children and Kathryn who is at her father's pocket, smiling fully.

"I have called Sherry to let her know we are here and where we are at," explains Samuel.

"Danki, Samuel," smiles Mary as she kisses Samuel again.

"Tonight, the kinner have their own room which adjoins ours, Susan and Ellie insist on having Christopher in the room with them. Ok?" Samuel is smiling broadly at Mary now.

"Let's unpack now," says Mary.

Clothes having been unpacked, and sandals being put on the children, a knock is heard on the door. Susan and Ellie enter, Susan with shorts and t-shirt and carrying her purse. Ellie is wearing her skirt as traditional with sandals on her feet the same ones bought while in Charleston.

"Nice sandals Ellie," looking down, Samuel smirks as Mary looks at Ellie's feet.

"Jah, Ellie when did you get sandals?" smiles Mary approvingly.

"Ach, Jah, I, in Charleston," responds a now very nervous Ellie.

Another knock on the door and everyone stops to look. Samuel takes hold of the knob and opens it up to Sherry and 3 children all dressed plain but not quite the same as their own children.

"Hello Mary," Sherry looks right past the small crowd gathering as Mary excited reaches through and hugs her friend.

"Sherry I got your mail, it is so good to see you, kinner kumme, meet my gut friend Sherry and her kinner, kumme, don't be shy," says Mary while reaching behind her and ushering three now shy children forward.

Joanna was the first to come up from Sherry and make the girls feel welcome, "Would you like to see the ocean with me," taking Rachel by the hand and smiling broadly. "I like to ride horses, have you ever ridden before?" she continued and making a connection the answer came excitedly.

"Jah, my daed has many horses and we have our own." Rachel looking up smiled also as she looked at Joanna and took her hand, "daed can we go down?"

"Jah," says Mary. "Wait for us though, we can all go together.

"Hi, I'm Sarah," taking hold of Kathryn's hand who is again very quiet but smiles at the kindness of Sarah, who is gentle.

Sherry's two girls are both taller and older than Mary's but take to each other readily as they move into the hallway. Only Taylor remained next to his mother and looking at Caleb.

Caleb picks up his hand timidly and just says, "Hi!"

"I've never seen the ocean before have you?" asks Caleb.

"Ah huh," says Taylor shaking his head.

A baby crying can now be heard as Ellie rushes away from the front door and Mary.

"Ach, your baby, let me see the baby," Sherry is smiling with a hint of a tear forming.

"Ellie has been such a help, I get more strength back each day. My life is so much better than it was. My headaches are gone. I feel gut!" Ellie comes out holding the baby from Mary's bed.

Sherry picks up the tiny bundle, pulling him close to her and taking in the fragrance of baby powder. She smiles and looks up momentarily, "I can never get tired of holding babies. They grow up so fast," as she pulls Christopher to her again. A tear falls.

"Well the kinner are looking forward to going out to the ocean, shall we, jah." Samuel smiles at everyone, looking around.

"I'll stay with the boppli," says Ellie.

"You want to see the ocean," says Mary.

"I have," answers Ellie.

"You have?" Samuel asks, surprised.

"Jah," a smile escapes just then as Susan can be seen smiling and looking away.

"Jah, gut, Lieutenant you know something."

Whipping around quickly, she replies holding in a chuckle, "Yes, sir!"

Laughing, Samuel shakes his head, "Ok ok, let's go...I have to hear about this sometime."

cccccccc

The ocean crashing could be heard getting closer as the families closed on the beach. Sand gave way beneath sandals as Sherry kicked her sandals off.

"Easier to walk on the beach with just your bare feet," she gestures to Mary.

"Jah," giggles Mary as she kicks off the sandals. She stops just for a moment and watches everyone else taking off their sandals. Burying her toes she feels the warmth wash over with every grain.

Closing her eyes she takes it in, and then begins to walk with her eyes closed opening them only after she feels the coolness of the water hit her feet. Lifting her arms up as if to catch her balance, she screams then laughs.

The girls holding up their dresses at first hold very still. Fearful at first, Kathryn asks, "Will the ocean take us away?" Everyone laughs except Joanna, who reaches and takes hold of Kathryn's hand.

"No, no you are ok, hold your dress, let me take your other hand, come run," she screams and the two now are running and splashing in the water.

Samuel rolls up the two boys pant legs, then his own and hollers, "Go! Go! Have fun! Jah! Have fun!

Susan walks along in her bare feet with purse slung over her shoulder and hands in her pocket looking around with a smile, when Samuel comes up from behind her.

"Sir," smiles Susan.

"Susan," says Samuel.

"We were bad, I was a totally bad influence on her, and it's my fault sir."

"Why does anything have to be at fault?" Asks Samuel who now walks next to her.

"We went out and I got her a bathing suit. I paid for it. Can't say I'm sorry."

"Did I say anything about being sorry?" Samuel looks down at her.

"No sir."

"Did you both have a good time, Ellie?"

"Yes sir, absolutely."

"Good, you both deserve to be happy," says Samuel sternly but with a smile.

Seagulls can now be heard; as they turn they watch as they dance amongst them. The gulls, diving down then up have the children chasing them back and forth.

Little arms can be seen waving back and forth, up and down. As all the adults watch grinning at little children and seagulls, Mary's eyes well...I thank thee Lord for these kinner, my husband, for Susan and Ellie and my gut friend Sherry, I thank thee Lord. I thank thee for my life...

cccccccc

Entering Sherry's home they feel the warmth of a family steeped in love.

"I have planned hand breaded pork chops, mashed potatoes and gravy. And for dessert I made 2 strawberry pies," she says as she looks down at all the children. The night went quickly and there would be one more day when the entire family would come together with Sherry and her family.

cccccccc

As with both the Fort Bragg trip and The Charleston trip, Samuel with Susan would leave for half a day for meetings which are not discussed with the family. The meeting in Charleston was at the Naval Base. This meeting would be at Mac Dill Air force base. Mary, Ellie and the rest of the family would spend the day relaxing at the hotel. Preparations are made for a long drive back.

cccccccc

"Lieutenant the plan will be to leave the car at MacDill for GSA to handle the pickup.

Willard N. Carpenter

The time is coming to an end, so...what is in store for you when you return to Bragg?"

"Sir, I don't know, rumor has it I'm up for a new assignment. They are beefing up security at some of the smaller bases around the country. And they are looking at me to help implement that."

"You're a good officer and leader. You'll do well where ever they send you. I have made arrangements with General Hutchins to have a letter of commendation placed in your personnel file."

"Thank you sir, so sir, how are we traveling north?"

"It's a surprise, we aren't driving," smiles Samuel looking over at Susan, now smiling herself.

"No arguments from me, certainly wasn't looking forward to that stretch."

"No too far. We fly out tomorrow."

Chapter Twenty-Four

The electronic whir from the clock sounded for the time set. It wasn't needed though because Christopher decided it was time to get up exactly 9 minutes before that. As if 6am wasn't early enough.

Ellie jumped up looking about as though startled. Getting up, having pulled on her robe she changed his diaper and began to think to herself, *Ach, you are so wet Christopher. You would think you emptied the ocean outside.*

"We have a long drive today I hope you don't act as a well's hand pump."

The diaper slid under his little bottom, and as his legs were lowered an amber stream went forth and came straight down the front of Ellie's night gown. "Ach, Christopher...where is all this coming from?" she chuckles.

"Ellie, what's up? Everything ok?"

"No, Christopher just wet on me," Ellie is laughing now, shaking her head no.

"Oh my I can hardly wait for this," remarks Susan sarcastically, smiling also. A knock can be heard at the door as Susan jumps up pulling on a robe.

"Guder mariye, Susan," says a sleepy Mary at the door.

"Good morning, for us, not for Ellie, Christopher peed on her," giggles Susan again.
"Ach, no...Ellie Wie gehts," asks Mary now entering the room.

"Ahh, I'm ok...just finishing, jah finished. There, Christopher your mama."

"Ahh my boppli," sighs Mary, lifting the small diapered form and into her bosoms close. Her lips meet the top of his head, dark and a muss. The light scent of baby powder can now be picked up in the room.

Susan peers out the window, taking in hints of the wind which moves the palms and waves. The wisps of broken white clouds move quickly by. On the horizon a ship can be seen just a speck even from her vantage.

Quickly she snaps around and taking a deep breath a tear can be seen by Mary.

"Susan, wie gehts?"

"I am going to miss you all so much," says Susan.

Ellie holding a towel in front of her moves quickly and embraces her.

"We will miss you also very much," comforts Ellie, now stepping back and taking hold of Susan's hand.

"Jah, we shall." She turns and quickly moves to the bathroom.

Voice breaking Elli continues, "I must remove this now. I'm beginning to smell like a wet Christopher, jah." A small cry is heard as the door closes behind her. It is overshadowed only by the shower water running.

Susan and Mary look at each other; the three women have become very close in the weeks since Mary's hospitalization.

"Mary, allow me to dress the little guy, Ok?"

"Jah, Susan, Danki."

cccccccc

"Samuel, where are we driving," asks Mary while sitting in the back with Samuel. Two hands are enmeshed; thumbs caress each others as they gaze lovingly into each other's eyes.

Mary's eyes now alone seek an answer.

"Last surprise, liebe," he says.

Mary continues to look, "Samuel, I think you should always be full of surprises. Another smile escapes her lips as she looks away and outside the vehicle.

Not much time passed when the black suburban carrying the Hersberger family for the last time passed through the entrance of Mac Dill Air force Base and into security.

Susan today wearing her battle dress uniform and Maroon Beret, shows her ID. Ellie is riding in front with Susan. Samuel opens his window and holds out his ID.

Samuel wears his BDU's with Green Beret a spread eagle in silver is attached to the berets striped flash.

"Sir, good morning...you are colonel Hersberger?"

"Yes sergeant, you should have me on your list," says Samuel with authority.

"Yes sir, you are to proceed to hanger one-zero-niner, sir. Drive straight ahead and go right at the T. Drive a half mile and find Lawrence Street on your left, this will take you to the hanger."

"Thank you, sergeant! Lieutenant, get that?"

"Yes sir!"

After a very short final drive the car pulls around and into the hanger where a small white straight wing jet awaited with the flight crew looking over the aircraft.

"Daed, what are we doing," asks Caleb with eyes very wide open.

"Ach, we are flying today," answers Samuel now imitating Caleb with his own eyes wide open while turning towards the back.

Now all the children are looking at their father excitedly as they get out of their seat belts and are on their knees oohing and ahhing...

cccccccc

With the family and Susan gathered at the foot of the C-21's steps. The aircrafts pilot steps up. "Sir, it's Major Casey, I flew you from Fort Bragg to Reading airport a little over a year ago."

"Major, yes I remember! Is this the same aircraft?" Samuel asks rubbing his hand over the fuselage.

"Actually, yes sir. Is this your family?" Samuel, looking to his left introduces the Air force major to everyone.

"I don't transport children to often. I bet you would like to see how this works huh?" Caleb was the first to answer, "Jah!"

"Come on you three, we can get loaded up a while."

Samuel looks at Mary now not saying a thing and with a curious look.

"The air force provides transportation for high ranking personnel with these C-21's. Since I'm down here on business for the last time, the general made sure we had transportation.

Inside the cockpit of the leer jet like aircraft, the co-pilot was already seated in the right seat, when Major Casey squeezed in with the children watching. Looking behind he has Caleb step forward. Caleb let's start this up, huh? Here flip this switch up.

Caleb on flipping the switch hears the whine of turbines begin. All three children look around in ah. The pilot and co-pilot look at each other and smile. They pull out their note book open it and begin their preflight check list as the co-pilot begins to look at the instruments.

Having placed the car seat in place and fastened young Christopher, now sleeping into it. The family, all but Samuel is fastened into the seats.

Coming forward Samuel stooping over a little speaks, "Major, we are ready."

"Yes sir, we'll have your children back up here once airborne, sir."

"Jah, whatever you think, Major."

"Sir, you must really have a story to tell."

"You would never believe it," laughs Samuel.

"Could be, could be..." agrees the major shaking his head and laughing.

"Captain let's bring up number two." The co-pilot hitting another switch and watching the gauges fastens his belts. The door of the small jet is closed with a small dull thud, as the click of locks from outside are heard.

The twin turbines pitch higher as the C-21 is directed straight out of the hanger by an airman with two lit wands in his hands over head waving the pilot out.

Once out of the hanger, the airman crosses the wands and the aircraft stops momentarily. The wand is pointed down ward.

The airman holding both wands now in his left hand salutes sharply and the aircraft taxies out toward the runway.

It is quiet in the aircraft when the pilot is given clearance for takeoff. Everyone is peering outside as the aircraft picks up speed as little bumps under the tires can be heard and felt. The feel and sound of the bumps get closer together then suddenly it lifts and everyone gasps.

"I love flying Samuel," says Mary while looking out the window. The landing gear can now be heard lifting and locking under the jet.

"What's that," asks Kathryn looking around.

"The wheels went inside the airplane," says Samuel looking around at Kathryn.

The C-21 having reached cruising altitude was now pointed at its first stop, when Major Casey came back.

Flight plan as follows, Fort Bragg for a drop off at Pope Air Force Base, Lieutenant that will be your stop. Then Mrs. Grau we are onto Ohio, to Wright-Patterson Air Force Base," says the Pilot when Samuel cuts in.

"Ellie, I have arranged a car to pick you up and transport you to your home."

"Then sir you and your family will arrive at Reading airport as we did before. You should be in this evening around 1800 hours this evening."

"Home, we are going home," says Mary with a longing in her eyes."

"Jah, home," reiterates Ellie with fear in hers.

"Colonel with your permission, you guys want to finish your tour of the cockpit?" the words were no sooner out of his mouth when Caleb was out of his seat. "Wait now, for your sisters."

He led them up and resumed his seat as the aircraft pointed straight out at wisps of clouds.

"What is that?" asks Rachel...

"Clouds we are flying into clouds," says the Pilot.

"Maam, yells Kathryn, we are driving into clouds." Everyone laughs now.

The clouds envelope the aircraft as the children look all around. As they pass from inside the cloud the pilot points out at the horizon, "the curve of the earth," he smiles back at them.

"Oooohhh..."

Chapter Twenty-Five

Colonel, we are on final approach to Pope Air force base. The small plane drops a little, making everyone look around at each other. Susan smiles and reaches across at her friend Ellie. "I will miss you my dear, dear friend," says Susan. "It has come time for me to get back to work."

The small plane touches down fast and hard lurching forward as it slowed quickly to a stop.

"Susan, you have come to be very special to us. Be well," says Samuel.

"Yes sir. Thank you," responds the young First Lieutenant. See those guys with beards and wearing jeans. Those are my people they are here to get you back home."

"Thank you again sir," says Susan being strong.

"Having hugged everyone goodbye, she leaves the small plane as the two bearded men salute sharply.

She can be seen returning their salute, then turning around one final time, this time not so strong and with a tear that she wipes away.

The Hersberger family, again airborne, watches out the window as Fort Bragg and the old Hersberger ranch off to the west pass by them. The family sit back a sigh can be heard from Mary. Christopher sleeps soundly. Rachel whimpers, "I miss Susan."

cccccccc

As the tires of the C21 touches the tarmac of a cool Air force runway in Ohio, Ellie Grau looks out the window. Smiling slightly she thinks back, *I will miss you. Yes Tom, I will miss you verra much.* Seeing Susan, a tear drops. *It's time to go home. To my farm to...my...husband.*

The brakes squeal. The small jet lurches forward, if only for a moment, when it begins its final taxi toward the hanger on a far side of the base. As the small white plane nears the hanger, a black limo with its driver awaits with ground crew and military police.

The copilot leaves his place in the right seat. As he unlocks the side door Samuel approaches Ellie. "Ahh Ellie, we are going to miss you," he says with more a smirk than smile.

They can hear the crew opening up the cargo door when the rest of the family stands up.

"We can all get off and stretch our legs now," says Samuel.

Kathryn can be heard crying, "Ellie I miss you!"

"I miss you too, already...kinner," cries Ellie, bending over and leaning on a seat weeps openly.

"Ach...Ellie, we will stay in touch, jah we will. Samuel has some things for you. Kumme, let's leave the plane."

As they reach the concrete of the hanger floor Samuel is bringing over a couple of boxes.

"I know some things, maybe I shouldn't, but I do. These are yours. Not your husbands. I heard that you want to write so I bought you a computer, a lap top. This should help you. It is already set up for use, I left instructions. Now this small box is a cell phone it is billed to me. You just use it."

Ellie looks up into Samuel's eyes choking back more tears shaking her head up and down. Samuel with Mary standing by his side lifts her head under her chin.

"Ellie, I know you have not been treated well by your husband. I know the rules. But Ellie you have our support. Do not let him hurt you. You call the number in here and we will always be around to help."

Ellie throwing herself into Samuels's arms weeps again. "Danki," she says softly as the driver takes the boxes from her, loading them into the trunk of the car. And in an instant everyone was sitting again in the small jet.

ccccccc

The small air force jet seemed like it reached cruising altitude quickly.

The cabin was very quiet with everyone staring out the window. Occasionally a whimper could be heard, then silence.

The flight from Ohio to Pennsylvania though not long in flight was longer in heart break. Mary occasionally looks over at her love. Thinking back to a time when she first woke up in an unfamiliar army hospital in an unknown city.

She remembers the first time she seen Samuel's face over a year ago in a familiar kitchen which she now calls her own. *How far we have journeyed my love and lover...How far we have journeyed. We have only just begun this life. I miss Ellie already and Susan. What a wonderful person. I miss our home and our life.*

For the last time Samuel feels the tires of a military plane touching the tarmac of the familiar surroundings of Reading Airport. He remembers past flights which had taken him into and out of combat.

A bitter sweet emotion over takes him, and as it does he looks around at his family and smiles, thinking to himself, *God is gut, jah, God is gut.*

The plane taxis up to the same area near the gate, more memories rush through his head as the same pilot is standing looking at him.

"Much different flight than the last, wouldn't you say sir?"

"Yes, it is. Nice flying and thank you for bringing my family and I home safely Major." He leans forward and taking the majors hand pulls him close and whispers, "Do me a favor...care for this military the way it has cared for me these many years major, I shall truly miss it."

"Yes sir, my pleasure." He pulls back and looks into the colonel's eyes, then looks down.

"Heh guys I have something for you." Opening his hands he produces little silver wings, pinning them on all the children. Little faces looks up at him smiling. "See just like mine."

A flat hand truck again is loaded. It is a de ja vue moment. Samuel with his family turns and looks back one more time. As he does the pilot and copilot come to attention and salute the Colonel. Samuel for the last time, with emotion slowly brings his right hand from his wife's and returns the salute.

It remains for what seemed to be the twenty years he spent within his countries service. He now flashes back to the many good times he had, to the many friends. His eyes lock with each of the officers standing opposite of him. Only they know what he is feeling.

His right hand came down slowly as his family looks on. Very briefly he remembers his first wife, smiles then looks at their daughter. Kathryn appearing confused, smiles up at her father.

cccccccc

Mary smiles as she grasps his right arm then reaches up and kisses his cheek. Samuel smiling reminds the major, "Remember."

"Sir, yes sir," says the major looking at the colonel wearing the Green Beret. "I'll remember."

cccccccc

The limousine proceeds down the same road as he had in a taxi not so long ago. The children sitting along the side enjoy the soda and snacks that were made available.

As they watch their children, their hand come together in longing as it had on a single date which started their adventure. Samuel turns to Mary and smiles and Mary remembers what he is thinking.

She brings her other hand up clutching his arm as she lays her head on his shoulder and they remember a dark quiet evening drive filled with longing, a longing which has been closed now.

cccccccc

Without fanfare the limo pulls into the blacktopped drive way of the Hersberger Ranch.

Mary sits up; *when I left...I don't remember leaving. It is gut to be home. Jah it is gut. Thank you Lord.*

Samuel looking over at his life, thinks to himself, *I feared this would not happen for one reason or the other. God is so gut. God is so gut.*

cccccccc

As the car doors open, a friend not seen from in a long time begins to appear.

First it is the familiar clip clop of horse hooves down the drive way as Mary screams out, "Uncle Samuel...Aunt Mary!"

"Woah," calls out a smiling Daniel.

195

Then his good friend Bill and Helen hearing the yelling are out on the porch of their house with a smile.

ccccccc

Bill, closing in on his friend, pauses at the sight in front of him as two ranch hands approach and stop short. The National Guard Sergeant and Specialist, quickly salute. "Sir, good evening!"

"Good evening boys, as you were," responds Samuel.

"Let me look at you," says Bill looking at his friend, "after all these years. Why didn't you say anything?"

"I'm sorry my good friend, I couldn't. I was with...I was with special operations."

"Well I'll be," responds Bill in disbelief reaching out and shaking his hand. "Anyhoot, welcome home."

ccccccc

Quiet has returned to the now nighttime of the Hersberger home, the children asleep alas in their own rooms. The baby now asleep after his last feeding is in the basinet.

Samuel looks into his wife's eyes, "Willkum home, liebe."

Bending over he goes to kiss her but not moving fast enough is met with Mary's warmth.

Her hands take his short hair, stroking her fingers through it as she opens her mouth again. She lowers her hands to his shirt buttons. One at a time they come apart as Samuel lets her hair fall. Then kissing her neck he traces back to her face quickly then he stops as their lips feel the moist breath of each other as though they would pause for an eternity.

Each breath consumes the others, they brush each other. Slowly the teasing gives way to breaths turning to the moistness of each other's passion.

The warmth of clothes is exchanged for clean sheets and blankets which envelopes passion bottled up by time.

cccccccc

The morning fog is met by Samuel out on the porch at day break. He lets Mary sleep in as he takes in the beauty of budding trees and spring flowers.

Again wearing what is traditional for his family, Samuel has retired his BDU's. He places his straw hat on his head, sips his coffee one more time and placing the cup on the table, begins a long walk.

Cutting through the mist of gray and white he comes across the cemetery. He walks down the path, a short cut from his farm. As he nears the not so lone marker a tear appears. They are not many anymore. He smiles a happy smile as he reaches his father's resting place amongst the white dewed grass. Looking down he remembers his father and him pulling his head toward his own. In a moment of tranquility his breath in a whiter fog escapes him as he says, "I have returned home, daed."

The Beginning!

Gentle Sun, Gentle Love

Gentle sun, my expression of love
Brightening the blue, in the sky of life
Allowing us to feel your emotion in the
     caressing wind
And softly glowing, so your warmth may mend
Gentle sun, I see your rays through clouds of
     strife

And when you sleep, you never go
Your light is with us in daughter moon
In brothers and sisters as they twinkle in a
     heavenly star
And when clouds do come, your brightness to
     mar
I will not worry, knowing I'll see you soon
     Gentle Sun, Gentle Love

Will

Dear Reader,

You Matter!

Simple words, yes, but they mean everything to me. I have taken the same attitude I have with my business and brought it here. At my business I always remember that I deal with people. They live, breath, smile, and cry about the same things I do. When they visit and order a sandwich, it is more than fueling up. Times are tough and I realize that if they are visiting me, they are looking for a treat, which means something special to them, especially if they visit with their families. So I shake hands and Thank and feed the troops. I thank a vet. I hand out lollies to children. And visit with my customers if they eat in. They matter!

Thus the same attitude is given when you read my e-book, book, or visit me on face book. You don't have to; your day is full like so many others. So if I am important enough for you to visit me, then you are important enough for me to respond to, in one form or another, to say, thank you!

The Lord's Blessings to you,
Will

About the Author

Will Carpenter is a faith filled family man, happily married for twenty-eight years.

His wife, Michele, is a nurse educator, Having been in nursing education for 25 years.

They have three children. Matthew a Lutheran pastor is married to Mandy a chaplain at the same church, they live in Michigan.

Lindsay presently lives outside of Seattle, Washington. She works in her dream job as a therapist using Applied Behavioral Analysis. She is married to Eli, a graduate of The Citadel and a U.S. Army officer. They were married this past June.

Mark their youngest is also a graduate of The Citadel; he graduated and commissioned into the Army this past May. He will attend flight school this spring at Ft. Rucker, Alabama. Mark, following flight school will be a medevac pilot, flying the UH-60 Blackhawk helicopter.

Mr. Carpenter spent eleven years in the Army as a medical specialist, army recruiter, army scout medic, and clinical specialist.

He completed his time in the military as the senior clinical specialist at the Battalion aid station of the 1st Battalion 111th Infantry. The country's oldest Infantry regiment formed under Benjamin Franklin.

He is also a retired nurse with twenty-nine years of experience in various settings to include areas of emergency medicine, pediatrics, geriatrics, and child and adolescent Psychiatry.

A business owner, he resides near Honey Brook, PA, an old order Amish community. This has enabled him to thoroughly research their deep-rooted faith and culture.

Keep in touch with Samuel and his family on Facebook.
http://www.facebook.com/people/Samuel-Hersberger/100001879866459

Keep in touch with the author.
http://www.facebook.com/Will1953

Website 'Secrets of the Son' Author Willard Carpenter
http://authorwillardcarpenter.com
(Other links can also be found here.)